the summer of cotton candy

To my husband, Scott, who loves theme parks even more than I do.

I would like to thank everyone who has helped me through the course of writing this book. Thank you to my parents and all my friends who listened as I described the theme park in detail. Thank you to my agent, Beth Jusino, for believing in me. Thank you to Barbara Scott and the group at Zonderkidz who championed the story. Thank you all.

A Sweet Seasons Novel

the summer of cotton candy

debbie viguié

ZONDERVAN®

ZONDERVAN.com/
AUTHORTRACKER
follow your favorite authors

We want to hear from you. Please send your comments about this book to us in care of zreview@zondervan.com. Thank you.

 **ZONDERVAN®**

The Summer of Cotton Candy
Copyright © 2008 by Debbie Viguié

Requests for information should be addressed to:

Zondervan, *Grand Rapids, Michigan 49530*

Library of Congress Cataloging-in-Publication Data: Applied for
ISBN 978-0-310-71558-0

Published in association with the literary agency of Alive Communications, Inc., 7680 Goddard Street, Suite 200, Colorado Springs, Colorado 80920. www.alivecommunications.com

Interior design by Christine Orejuela-Winkelman

Printed in the United States of America

08 09 10 11 12 • 25 24 23 22 21 20 19 18 17 16 15 14 13 12 11 10 9 8 7 6 5 4 3 2 1

the summer of cotton candy

1

Candace Thompson wondered where her life had gone wrong. Maybe when she was fourteen, she should have babysat her bratty cousin when her parents asked. Maybe when she was seven, if she hadn't locked the teacher out of the classroom, this wouldn't be happening to her. No, maybe her life went all wrong when she was three and she knocked down the girl with the pigtails who had stolen Mr. Huggles, her stuffed bear. Yes, the more she thought about it, that must have been the moment that started her on the path that led to the special punishment she was now suffering.

It was the first day of summer vacation, but for Candace, it might as well have been the last. She sat in a dark dreary office, signing away her freedom. The decree had come down from her father: she had to get a job. No job, no cash. No cash, no movies or hanging with her friends. It didn't matter to him that if she had a job she wouldn't have time to do the things she would need the money for.

She took a deep breath as she finished filling out the last form and handed it across the desk to the recruiter, Lloyd Peterson, a strange-looking man in a frumpy brown suit whom she was convinced had to be a perv. Hadn't she seen him on

America's Most Wanted? She slid down into her seat, willing herself to be invisible, or at least small enough to slip away unnoticed.

"Candace," he mused, "can I call you Candy?"

"Well …" She was about to say no. She hated that name.

"Great. So, Candy, what makes you want to work for The Zone?"

She didn't want to work for The Zone, she just wanted to enjoy her summer like everybody else. Her father had put his foot down, though. According to him it was time she learned the value of work and earning her own way. She had chosen to work for The Zone because she had absolutely no skills, and working for a theme park seemed more interesting than flipping burgers.

She sighed and squirmed, refusing to meet the recruiter's eyes. "I've always dreamed of working for The Zone. I want to be part of the excitement and help people enjoy themselves more." It was her rehearsed answer, and she held her breath, hoping he would buy it.

He stared at her for a long minute before nodding. Picking up a bright blue folder on his desk, he flipped it open and cleared his throat. "You realize, of course, that if you wanted a summer job, you should have started applying months ago, right?" he asked, staring at her over the tops of his glasses.

She slunk farther down into her chair. She licked her lips when she realized he expected an answer. "No," she said.

"No? No? Well, you are wrong. In order to get a good summer job, you should start applying at least in March."

March! All I could think of in March was holding out until spring break without going postal. Her eyes were now nearly level with the edge of his desk. "I just thought, you know, The Zone needs a lot of employees."

"You are correct, but most of our summer positions have already been filled."

He stopped and stared at her. She wasn't sure what he expected her to say, but she was beginning to have the sinking feeling that her summer would consist of asking people if they wanted fries with their meal.

Just as she was about to get up to leave, sure that the interview had come to an end, he spoke. "We do, however, have two openings."

She sat up. "What are they?"

"The first is janitorial."

"You mean those people who go around sweeping up after everyone?" *That might not be so bad. At least I could keep moving, and nobody ever pays attention to them.*

He raised an eyebrow. "Some of our janitorial employees do that, but not this position. This one is cleaning up the women's restrooms."

Candace's stomach turned. In her mind she pictured the high-school bathroom by fourth period, and that was only with a few hundred users, not thousands. There was no way she was going there.

"Um, and the other one is …?" she managed to ask as diplomatically as she could.

"Cotton candy operator."

"I'll take it!" she exclaimed, more loudly than she had meant to.

"Good!" Lloyd stood up and opened a drawer in one of his many filing cabinets. He pulled out a stack of papers two inches thick and slammed them down on his desk right in front of her. The desk continued to shake for a moment as though there had just been an earthquake. "Fill those out."

"Now?" she asked, her mind boggling over the enormity of the task. She moved slightly so that she was eye level with the stack, and she could feel her hand begin to cramp up in premature protest.

"Yes, now. You can, however, use the table in the courtyard if you'd be more comfortable."

The word *duh* came to mind, but she bit her tongue and kept it to herself.

"Yes, sir, thank you. I'll do that," she said instead, scrambling to her feet and grabbing the stack of papers. She made her way out of the room as fast as she could, taking a deep breath once in the hallway.

The hallways around this place are roomier than the offices, she thought to herself as she immediately began to feel less claustrophobic. She turned around, not sure which way the courtyard would be. She hadn't seen one on her way in, so it must be in the other direction.

She came to a T in the hall and craned her neck to the right. All she could see that way were more offices, so she turned to the left ...

... and ran straight into a six-foot wall.

"Umph," the wall gasped as Candace's papers went flying in all directions.

"I am so sorry," Candace said, realizing that the wall she had run into was actually a guy, a *big* guy, a guy with muscles she could see through his shirt. She looked up and forgot what she was going to say next. She was staring at the Lone Ranger. He stood there, larger than life in pale blue, complete with boots and gun belt. Black wavy hair shone from underneath a white hat pushed far back on his head. A black mask covered part of his face.

All this was not what stopped her in her tracks, though. What took her breath away and caused her to stare like an idiot were his eyes. He had amazing eyes that were bright blue and crackled like lightning. He stared right through her, and her heart began to hammer.

"I—I—"

He smiled at her, and she felt dizzy. "Are you lost, my lady?"

She nodded, still unable to look away from those piercing eyes.

"Here, let me help you," he said, bending down.

For one dizzying moment his face came close to hers, and she thought he was going to kiss her just like in some movie.

Instead of kissing her, though, he knelt down and began picking up her papers.

Idiot, she said to herself, feeling her cheeks burning. Her knees began to buckle, and she covered it by quickly dropping down to her knees and scooping up some of the papers that had managed to spread themselves across the width of the hall.

"I'm such a klutz," she said.

"Not at all. How could you expect to run into something when you're not looking where you're going?"

She glanced up quickly, stunned at the rebuke. Then she noticed that he was grinning from ear to ear. They both burst out laughing.

"That should do it," he said finally, handing her the last sheet of paper. His fingers brushed hers, and she felt her stomach do a flip-flop.

"Thanks."

"So, where are you headed?"

"Um, um," she stammered for a moment, her mind going completely blank.

"I take it you're filling these out?" he said, tapping the stack of papers.

She nodded, relieved as she remembered, "Something was said about a courtyard that had a table."

"I'll show you where it is."

She fell into step with him, and he led her down the corridor. They made three quick turns in a row and arrived at a door leading out to what truly was a small courtyard.

"There you go," he said, holding the door open for her. She walked outside into the sun and plunked her papers down onto a table.

"Thanks."

"I live to serve."

She couldn't think of something witty to say, so she just stared at him.

He winked at her. "I'll see you around."

Then he turned and left. She sank down into the chair, her knees feeling weak. "Who was that masked man?"

Four hours and three phone calls to her father later, Candace finished filling out the application. She stacked up the tax forms, identity forms, nondisclosure forms, noncompetition agreements, and receipt-of-employee-handbook forms. And with a snort, she put the background check and financial disclosure form on top of the whole stack. She was seventeen, and she had no finances to disclose. She'd had a momentary panic about the background check until she realized they were looking for things like a criminal background or drug use and wouldn't be interested in the fact that she'd had detention twice in seventh grade.

She flipped back through the employee handbook. It was over a hundred pages long. After reading through it, she realized that The Zone had a policy and procedure for absolutely everything. They even had three different emergency-evacuation plans, depending on whether it was fire, weapons problems, or natural disasters. Clearly the people who worked on the handbook were paranoid, and now, after reading it, so was she.

She dragged herself to her feet, her stomach angrily reminding her that lunch had been hours before and she had missed it. She miraculously made her way back through the maze of corridors to Mr. Peterson's office. He was speaking on the phone, so she stood in the doorway until he looked up and saw her.

He hung up the phone. "Come in, Candy. I take it you're done?"

She nodded, handing him the stack.

"Excellent. Well, I'll take a look at all these. I'm sure they're in order. Let me just get copies of your driver's license and social security card."

She fished them out of her purse and handed them to him. He left the office for a minute and then returned with photocopies. He handed her cards back to her.

"Okay, you'll start orientation tomorrow."

"Tomorrow?" she asked.

"Yes, is there a problem with that?" he asked sharply.

"I just thought I'd have a couple of days before—"

"Tomorrow's our last orientation class for the summer. It's either tomorrow or never."

Never *wasn't* an option, no matter how much she wanted it to be. A vision of a certain masked man flitted briefly through her mind. Then again, maybe this wasn't going to be so bad after all.

"Tomorrow. Tomorrow is fine for me," she said.

"Report to the lobby at seven forty a.m."

There went any hope she had of sleeping in, probably forever. She sighed and nodded.

"What do you mean you have to be home early tonight?" Candace's best friend, Tamara Wilcox, huffed over the phone. "I thought we were hanging out?"

"We can still hang. I just need to get some sleep. I have to start work early in the morning," Candace explained. She flipped onto her back and braced her legs against the wall next to her bed.

There was only silence on the other end of the phone.

"Tam, you still there?"

"Uh-huh. Meet me at Starbucks."

"Can't. I'm getting a job to earn summer spending money, and Dad won't give me an advance."

"I'm buying. Just get your butt over here."

Ten minutes later Candace was sitting down at a corner table where Tamara was already waiting for her. Without a word, Tamara slid a grande hot chocolate with a shot of raspberry across the table to her.

Candace blew through the tiny opening in the lid like she always did. Tonight, though, the whistling sound it produced didn't make her smile. She was too busy trying to avoid looking at the daggers in Tamara's eyes.

"So, you're ditching me for the summer?"

"No, just five days a week. I should be free evenings and weekends."

"Did they guarantee that?"

"Well, no, but they said it would likely be that. They couldn't expect me to work during church, you know?"

Tamara crossed her arms over her chest, a sure sign she wasn't buying it. "And what about youth group? Even if they don't make you work Sunday morning they're going to make you work Friday nights."

"I should be free evenings," Candace said, slinking down into her seat and hating that she was repeating herself. Somehow, it sounded less plausible than it had earlier in the recruiter's office.

"And if you're not? It's bad enough you're going to be blowing off church and youth group, but what about me? I'm your best friend. What kind of summer am I going to have without you?"

"Come on, no matter what hours I get, it will only be thirty-five a week. We can still do all kinds of stuff. And I'll have the money to pay for it," Candace said with a sigh. It was amazing sometimes how Tamara could turn anyone's pain into her own.

Tamara uncrossed her arms and leaned forward, tapping one perfectly manicured nail on the table. "You know, if money is the issue, I can take care of that."

Candace stared at her. Tamara was rich. Her whole family was. Her monthly allowance was more than some people made in a year. Candace knew she was serious, and it was a tempting offer.

"I can't," she said at last, tears of frustration filling her eyes. "My dad would kill me."

Tamara sat back, a disappointed look on her face. "Oh, is he pulling that rite-of-passage, learn-the-value-of-work crap on you?"

Candace nodded and wiped her eyes with the back of her hand. "Yeah, he'd freak if I backed out. And I don't think you're prepared to pay for my college tuition."

Tamara laughed. "Would it get you to bail on this whole Zone thing?"

Candace scowled. "He's my dad. What can I do?"

"Nothing," Tamara said, shaking her head. "Parents are so much work."

2

The next morning at 7:42 a.m. Candace was wishing she had taken Tamara up on her offer. She stood with two dozen others as the early morning sun shone in their eyes. A short, wide man with a name tag that read *Jay* paced before them, extolling the virtues of working for The Zone. She could swear she saw flecks of foam at the corners of his mouth.

In her hands Candace held another bundle of information that she was expected to familiarize herself with. She also had her name tag. She twisted it back and forth, refusing to put it on. At last Jay noticed.

"Miss, is there a problem? You should be wearing your name tag."

"Well, I would, but it says *Candy*, and that's not my name," she explained.

"What is your name?"

"Candace."

"Close enough. Put it on."

"But—"

"Before you go home you can fill out a form to get a new name tag, but for now, wear it." He accompanied the order with a glare.

Grimacing, Candace pinned it on her blouse over her heart. The blonde girl standing next to her leaned closer and whispered, "It could be worse. At least they got part of your name right."

Candace glanced at her name tag. "Mary?"

"Not even," the blonde answered. "Try Sue."

"Bummer."

"Tell me about it. Where are you working?"

"Cotton candy operator," Candace whispered.

"Nice. I got janitorial—women's restrooms."

Candace struggled to keep her expression neutral. "It could be worse."

"No, it really couldn't. I came in yesterday afternoon, and it was the last job open."

Candace was suddenly very grateful that she had gone in to see the recruiter *before* eating lunch.

After a minute, she realized that the group was moving. She hastened to follow, surprised that Jay could move so quickly. He led them at a breakneck pace around the vast areas behind the scenes where only employees were allowed to go, also known as "off field."

Just when she was good and lost, Jay led the group to a halt in front of an unassuming door. "All right, bunch up everyone. Smile, and remember you represent The Zone. Keep together and keep up."

He opened the door and they all walked through it ... and into the park. Candace looked around in amazement. They had just walked through a door she had never noticed before in the back of the park in the Extreme Zone. Directly in front of her a bungee jumper dropped screaming from the sky.

She flinched, and out of the corner of her eye she saw others do the same.

"It's like a miracle!" someone nearby squeaked. "We're here, and we didn't even go through the front gate!"

"Yes, it's just one of the many miracles you'll experience working at The Zone," Jay said, without even a hint of sarcasm.

It creeped Candace out, the way Jay and some of the others acted, like The Zone was some sort of shrine to the god of entertainment. Worse than that, it was their holy grail.

She shrugged it off and tried to pay attention to what Jay was saying. "... as you all should know, the theme park is divided into eight areas, or zones. There's the Kids Zone, where the kiddie rides are. The History Zone covers many different time periods and famous people, both real and fictional. The Thrill Zone hosts all the roller coasters and big rides. The Extreme Zone is for extreme sports and activities, such as our bungee-jump attraction. The Splash Zone is full of water rides. The Exploration Zone is where you can find all the science-related rides and activities. The Holiday Zone is our seasonal holiday-themed area, and right now it's a celebration of the Fourth of July. The Game Zone includes all our traditional sports activities, including our batting cages and carnival games. Leading to the eight zones is the Home Stretch, which includes the main gate and the shops in the front of the park."

None of this was news to Candace. Her family had been going to The Zone at least once a year for as long as she could remember. She knew that the park had been created by a retired football star, hence the sports terminology.

"And what do we call the exit?" Jay asked.

"End Zone," Candace answered with everyone else.

Candace felt self-conscious as they walked through the park. Everywhere they went people stared and pointed, many in admiration. Candace felt herself turning red. Attention was something she usually liked to avoid. That was one of the great things about being friends with Tamara—all eyes usually gravitated toward her and away from Candace. That was how Candace liked it.

The group continued to walk, and Candace forced her eyes forward. *Just keep walking*, she told herself. They wound their way through each zone, Jay talking endlessly about things that Candace hoped she wouldn't be quizzed about later.

At last the tour was over, and they returned to the off-field area. They found their way to the Locker Room, which was the area where she would start each day. The Locker Room held lockers, time clocks, notices, and boxes where new schedules were put out. There Candace came upon her second surprise of the day when she picked up her schedule. She stared at it unbelievingly.

"Sundays, Tuesdays, and Thursdays eight thirty to five o'clock. Fridays and Saturdays one thirty to nine o'clock!"

She ran over to Jay and showed it to him. "This is wrong. I was told I'd be working weekdays. I have church on Sundays. I don't even have two consecutive days off! And besides, the hours aren't even consistent."

Jay laughed and a chill went through her. "I don't know what you were told, but you work the hours you're needed. Schedules change every two weeks. You're free to request specific days and hours, but being that you're new here, you pretty much get whatever's left over. Be grateful you're not stuck with a closing shift and then an opening shift back-to-back ... yet."

He turned and walked away to answer someone else's question. Candace continued to stare at her card. *This isn't happening!* she thought, panicking. By the time she got home on Fridays, she would just have time to eat dinner before going to bed. No youth group for her. And working on Saturdays! She might as well kiss her dreams of a social life good-bye.

She had one faint hope, though. She pulled her cell out and called her dad.

"Dad! They have me working Sundays during church! They won't let me out of it," she told him.

"I'm sorry, Candace, but if that's your schedule, I guess there's nothing to do about it. You could always go to evening services," he suggested.

"Thanks, Dad," she said, her last chance at escaping her summer prison evaporating before her eyes.

After visiting the wardrobe department and getting her uniform, Candace drove slowly home. She tried Tamara's cell for
the fifth time, hoping her friend would pick up.

"Hello?" Tamara asked.

Candace tried to speak, but burst into tears instead.

"Candace, is that you?"

She blubbered something that vaguely resembled a yes.

"I'll be home in five minutes. Meet me there," Tamara
instructed.

Candace hung up and tried to dash away her tears. Driving
while crying was never a good idea.

Once in Tamara's room, Candace broke down completely.
She handed Tamara the copy of her schedule and just cried in
misery. After a minute, Tamara put her arms around her.

"Quit, Cand, just quit. We'll work something out."

"I can't!"

"Listen, don't cry. It's going to be okay. This schedule isn't so
bad. You'll be free all day Monday and all day Wednesday. We
can do stuff those days."

Candace dried her tears. "I'm sorry, Tam. I just feel trapped,
you know?"

Tamara laughed. "Boy, do I ever," she said, glancing around
her room.

Candace laughed, remembering when Tamara's father had
hired a private investigator to follow a guy Tamara wanted to go
out with. It had been funny to Candace, but she remembered
how upset Tamara had been. She had given her father the silent
treatment for a month over that one.

"Okay, okay, so you get the whole trapped part. It's just, if
this is what growing up is like, I don't want to."

"There are worse things than growing up," Tamara said.

"Name one," Candace challenged.

"Having your father tell you who you can and cannot date."

"You win," Candace said with a laugh.

"There you go. So what if you're working a few hours every week. Maybe it will be kind of fun."

"Maybe," Candace answered, even though she didn't feel sure about it.

"Enough of that, let's figure out what we're going to do tomorrow to celebrate your job."

"Don't you mean mourn my loss of freedom?"

Tamara shrugged, "Half full, half empty—it doesn't matter. It's the same glass of water."

Candace laughed, beginning to feel better.

"All right, what are we going to do? Money is no object. It's my treat."

Candace grinned. "No object?"

"No object," Tamara said firmly.

The next day they road-tripped to Northgate, their favorite mall. It was a two-hour drive from home. By the time they parked, Candace was already feeling optimistic about the future. Shopping, or even the potential for shopping, could do that.

Tamara wrinkled her nose. "Mom made me promise I'd pick up something for her in Bloomy's."

Candace shook her head, "When I start getting paid, I still won't be able to afford to even breathe in that place."

"Please, how many times do I have to tell you? The air in Bloomy's is free. If you want to pay for such things, you'll have to go to the Oxygen Bar."

"You know I don't trust air I can't see," Candace joked.

Tamara rolled her eyes. "Isn't your mom supposed to be some sort of environmental activist?"

"Something like that," Candace said. "She hates it when I say things like that."

"I'll bet." Tamara lowered her voice, "The hottie at the pretzel counter is totally checking you out."

"As if! He's scoping you. You're the real scenery."

"Stop dragging yourself down, Cand. You're every bit as pretty as I am. You just need to put the 'tude with it. Then you'll have to scrape them off."

Candace smiled. *I don't think I'll ever turn heads like Tamara. Besides, I only need to turn one head.* She stopped, startled when she realized she was thinking again of the guy in the Lone Ranger costume. *I wonder if I'll see him around the park? I wonder if he'll remember me?*

She shook her head. *This is crazy! I'm thinking about some guy whose face I haven't even seen. How pathetic is that?*

"What is it?" Tamara asked.

"Nothing," Candace said, unwilling to share her fantasies about a mystery man she'd probably never see again. *He probably doesn't even have close to the same schedule that I do.*

The day went by too quickly, but in the end Candace had three new outfits to show for it, all thanks to Tamara. As they were driving home, Candace fell silent, thinking about the money that had been spent.

"What is it?" Tamara asked.

"I just feel bad, taking advantage of you like that."

"Advantage, how?" Tamara asked, sounding genuinely puzzled.

"The clothes."

"Stop it," Tamara snapped, her voice louder than usual. It made Candace jump, startled.

"Look," Tamara continued, her voice softer. "We've been friends since before money meant anything to either of us. So, I know it's not about that. I know where I stand with you. That's why I don't have a problem paying for stuff for you too. It wouldn't be as much fun shopping by myself or being the only one getting things."

"Thanks," Candace said.

"So, no more feeling guilty?"

"No more."

"Does this mean you'll quit your job?"

"No."

"Dang it!" Tamara said, pounding her fist into the steering wheel. "Oh well, can't blame me for trying."

That night Candace added her job to the list of things that she usually prayed for. Still, she felt uneasy and tossed and turned for hours, stressing about starting work in the morning. She whispered another prayer, begging for peace and enough sleep to make it through her first day. Then she crushed Mr. Huggles to her chest. She still slept with him, especially when she was stressed about something. "What do you think?" she asked the teddy bear.

He was his characteristically silent, but supportive, self. She kissed his nose and closed her eyes, desperately hoping for sleep.

3

She was standing behind her cart, her name tag pinned crook-
edly on her striped pink and white blouse. A line of people a
mile long stood clamoring for cotton candy, their voices grow-
ing louder every second. At last she clapped her hands over her
ears. Too late she realized that she had just matted her hair with
sticky pink sugar. She began to back away from the cart, wishing
she knew where a bathroom was.

"Hey there, lady," a voice behind her said.

She twisted around and saw the Lone Ranger, standing with
his hat in his hand. She stood gaping, sticky hands pressed to
sticky hair.

"You know, you shouldn't go outside without your pants on."

"What are you talking about?" she shouted.

Then he began to laugh. Everyone was laughing. She
could hear the roar through hands and sugar and hair. Finally,
she looked down and realized that she was completely naked
from the waist down. She screamed and tried to run. Globs of
sticky pink goo oozed around her feet, making them stick to
the ground. She tried to move her hands to cover herself, but
they were stuck to her hair. She screamed again and began
to cry.

She heard another voice and turned her head to see the recruiter leering at her from behind his desk. "You know, you should have started dressing hours ago. You need to wake up now."

Suddenly she woke and saw her mother staring at her. "Candace, you're late, you should have already been dressed."

"Late for what, Mom?" she asked, still not sure where she was.

"Work, you should have left five minutes ago."

"Work? Work!" she shouted and launched herself out of the bed, tripping when her left foot tangled in the sheets. She fell onto the floor in a pile of blankets.

"Help me!"

Her mother just raised an eyebrow. "It's your job, your responsibility. You have to sink—"

"Or swim on my own," Candace finished in disgust. She had heard that all her life, and she swore that if she heard it one more time she was going to lose it.

"So swim already," her mother said, sarcasm dusting her voice. "I'm off to work."

Candace sat for a moment, frustrated and out of breath. When she heard the door close downstairs, she scrambled to her feet and raced to the bathroom. She grabbed her makeup kit and dashed a bit of blush across her cheekbones. Her hand shook as she applied a pale pink lipstick to her lips.

She threw on her pink-striped blouse and white skirt. She ruined two pairs of nylons before she finally managed to get a pair all the way up. She slipped on her white shoes that reminded her of the ones the school nurse wore. The pin on her name tag stabbed her as she tried to push it through her shirt. She bit her lip and hoped that she wasn't bleeding, but she didn't have time to check. She grabbed her purse and flew out the door.

Forty-five minutes after she woke up, she was standing behind her cart in the Kids Zone with a fake grin plastered on. Martha, a wizened old woman with a smoker's cough, was her trainer. Actually Martha was a manager, but apparently the trainer was out sick.

The Kids Zone had to be the most chaotic part of the park. There were a few traditional rides where kids would board vehicles and wind through tableaus from classic stories like The Little Mermaid, Princess and the Pea, and Little Red Riding Hood. For Little Red Riding Hood, the ride cars were shaped like baskets of goodies, and for Princess and the Pea, they looked like a giant stack of mattresses. A lot of the other games and rides, though, were far less contained. There was a huge finger-painting wall that started out white every morning and ended each day a mess of color. There were ball pits in several places. A huge set of tubes, like the Habitrail you'd see on a hamster's cage, wound around the tops of several of the build-ings, and you could see kids happily climbing and sliding all day long. A foresty maze with a gingerbread house in the center al-ways reverberated with lots of high-pitched squeals of laughter. Perhaps messiest and craziest of all the games was Silly String Tag, a messy version of Laser Tag that had kids pouring out of the building, trailing Silly String everywhere. She didn't know how the janitors kept up with it all.

"All righty, missy, you think you got it?" Martha asked after an hour. Candace nodded, her mouth too dry to speak. Martha stepped back to let Candace handle the next customer.

The sun came out with a vengeance, and scorched the black pavement. Candace's red curls were plastered to her head, and she could feel sweat rolling down the small of her back. Her fingers were sticky from the cotton candy, and the background music that played on continuous loop in the Kids Zone was starting to drive her insane. The music was a high, tinny instru-mental version of "I Want Candy." She figured it was meant as a subliminal message to kids already hyped up on sugar to beg their parents for more.

Several feet away, a man seemed to be arguing with his wife as his two little boys jumped up and down between them. At last, the man separated himself from his family and walked up to her cart.

She plastered a smile on her face. "Hello, sir, what can I get for you?"

He stared at her for a moment, and then a sly smile spread across his face. "Candy," he answered, letting her know with his eyes that he wasn't talking about the sticky sugary stuff that was coating her hands.

Eew! Gross, she thought. He just kept staring at her, and she dropped her eyes. "Pink or green?" she asked.

"Pink," he said, his voice still slimy sounding. She blushed until she was sure her cheeks must match her hair.

"Three dollars," she told him.

She flinched as he tried to hold her hand for a moment as he gave her the money. She thanked God silently that the man had given her three ones and that she wouldn't have to give him change.

"Here you go," she said, picking up a paper cone already wrapped in sticky pink goodness. She practically threw it at him and refused to meet his eyes. She heaved a sigh of relief when he walked away.

Martha made a clucking sound. "You'll find there's more where he came from, but you did good. Just remember, there's an intercom under the counter. Hit the red panic button if someone gives you too much trouble, and security will be here before you know it."

"Has anyone ever had to hit the panic button?" Candace asked.

Martha snorted. "Only about once a month."

Candace stared at her in dismay. Martha patted her shoulder. "Don't worry, you'll get used to it."

Candace opened her mouth to assert the fact that she most certainly would *not* get used to it. But before she could say anything, Martha glanced at her watch.

"I've got to go open somewhere else. There's more demand for snack food starting around this time of day. I'm sorry I don't have more time. Hopefully the trainer will be back in tomorrow, and she can walk you through anything else you need to know. You're going to be fine. Someone should be by in a few minutes to give you your break."

Then Martha took off, leaving Candace all alone. *Just breathe*, she told herself. *Someone will be here soon, and you can take a break. Everything's going to be okay.*

Except no one came to give her a break. She squirmed, not knowing what to do. She didn't have keys to lock everything up, and she couldn't just leave the stand—including the cash box—unattended. So she waited, and the minutes ticked by painfully.

By the time she was relieved for lunch, she was exhausted. She limped to the nearest exit and made her way to the employee cafeteria.

There she grabbed a turkey sandwich and a bottle of water and sat down gratefully on a bench. She drank half the water in a matter of seconds and then just sat for a few minutes staring at the sandwich.

"First day?" a voice beside her asked.

She turned and looked up. "Zorro?" she asked.

"*Sí, senorita*," he said, bowing with a flourish and putting on a thick accent.

She looked deep into his eyes, once again framed by a mask, and recognized that it must be the Lone Ranger from the recruiting office.

"Is it that obvious?"

He nodded. "Even if I hadn't seen you the other day at HR. You can always spot new refs—they're the ones that look half dead."

"Refs?" she asked, more interested in staring into his eyes than hearing what he was saying.

He laughed. "Referee, remember? Employees are called referees and customers are called players?"

"That's right," she said, blushing furiously. *He must think I'm a total idiot*, she thought.

"Don't worry. If you can last the week, you'll be fine."

"I hope so."

"You will," he assured her. He resumed with an accent, "Zorro gives you his word."

He drew his sword, saluted her, and then turned and swept away, cape fluttering in the wind.

She just sat and stared after him.

Lunch was over before she knew it, and she limped back to her cart. Without a word, the girl who had been minding it left, her pace brisk. Candace got out some empty paper cones and began to roll them, one after another, inside the spinning tub. The cotton candy wound itself onto the cones like webbing wrapping itself around a spider's helpless victim.

After half an hour of that, Candace realized that thin strands of cotton candy were stuck to her clothes. She must have caught some accidentally on her arm or sleeve. She shook her clothes, trying to get it off, but it just clung more fiercely.

"Hey there."

She looked up, embarrassed at being caught unaware. A guy that looked like a surfer, right down to the baggy shorts and bleached white hair, was smiling at her. The only thing that gave him away as a ref was a name tag—Josh—worn on a tank top with a subtle blue stripe in it.

"I work at the Kowabunga ride."

"The Splash Zone," Candace said with a smile.

"That's right."

"Nice uniform," she said with a wistful smile, thinking that what he was wearing was probably a lot cooler than hers.

"It's one of the best in the park." He leaned closer conspiratorially. "That's why there's a waiting list to work there."

"How did you get it?" she asked, curious.

He smiled. "I applied in March."

Duh! She felt like slapping her forehead, but restrained herself.

"They had me work part-time until last week."

"Didn't it rain like the entire month of March?" she asked.

"Yeah, storms nearly every day," he affirmed.

"You had to have been freezing!"

"I was, but it was worth it to not sweat away the summer."

She laughed. "Good choice."

"Yeah, your cotton "candy-striper" look is cute, but it has to be hot."

"Thank you, I thought I was the only one who noticed. I feel like I should be working in a hospital."

He laughed, a nice, easy sound. "Well, I got to get back to my post." He glanced at her name tag and his eyes widened. "Candy," he said and started laughing even harder. "I'm sorry, that's just really unfortunate."

"It's worse than that. My name is Candace. I hate Candy."

He slapped his thigh. "Of course you do. It took me three weeks to get them to put Josh on my name tag instead of Joshua. Not even my parents call me that."

"Only three weeks?" she teased. "Then maybe there's hope for me."

"Oh, there's always hope. Catch you later, Cotton *Candace*." He waved and took off.

The next hour dragged by. The good part was that she was busier than she had been all morning, but it wasn't enough to completely distract her from the heat and the pain in her feet. *I never knew standing could be such hard work.*

She was just coming up on her afternoon break, a much anticipated event, when she looked up and saw Tamara walking toward her, a triumphant smile on her face.

"Tamara! What are you doing here?"

"Since you couldn't hang with me, I thought I'd come hang with you," Tamara said. "I've been to every cotton candy stand in the park looking for you."

"Tam, that was sweet, but you don't have to do this."

"I do now."

"Why?" Candace asked, confused.

Tamara whipped a card out of her pocket. "Because, thanks to you, I'm now a season-ticket holder, and I plan on getting my two hundred dollars' worth."

"You're the best."

"I know. So, do they give you breaks or what?"

Candace waved to a girl headed her way dressed as she was. "I've got my afternoon break right now."

"Good on me. I couldn't have better timing."

"Your timing rocks," Candace confirmed as she gratefully relinquished her post.

"So, where do the fine guys work around here?"

"I can think of one place," Candace said with a blush.

"Lead the way."

They walked across to the History Zone, which would be more accurately named Somebody's Fantasy of What History Should Be Zone. In it, cowboys mingled with knights. King Tut rubbed shoulders with superheroes. Candace, however, ignored all of them and looked for a particular black-clad swordsman.

"Howdy, ma'am," a gunfighter said, tipping his hat as he paused in front of them.

"Check again," Tamara said. "It's *mademoiselle*. I'm too young to be a madam."

"My apologies, *mademoiselle*, it was a slip of the tongue," he said, giving her a wink.

He continued walking down the street and Tamara turned to stare after him.

Just then, Candace spotted her target and grabbed Tamara's arm before she knew what she was doing.

"Who?" Tamara asked, swinging her head around. "Zorro?"

Candace nodded.

"He's built."

"Tell me about it."

"Ah, so I take it you know this Zorro?"

"Not exactly. I've seen him a couple times, though."

"So, you're crushing."

"Affirmative."

Zorro did a slow spin in the street, showing off for some tourists.

"Definitely crush worthy," Tamara noted.

Zorro turned toward them and nodded, flashing a smile at Candace. She felt her heart skip a beat even as she forced herself to wave nonchalantly.

Tamara was staring at her. "Now I get why you wanted to work here."

"No," Candace said with a smile. "He's just one of the perks."

4

It was Friday, her second day of work, and although Candace had woken up with her alarm, run a few errands for her mom, and gotten to work on time, she still wandered around for twenty minutes unable to find her cart. She had started in the Kids Zone where the cart had been the day before. The spot where it stood was empty. A referee who worked at the Painting Wall told her it had rolled on toward the Thrill Zone earlier that morning.

In the Thrill Zone, a referee at the Rimshot Coaster pointed her toward the Extreme Zone. When she hadn't seen the cotton candy cart in the Extreme Zone she'd continued on into the Splash Zone, where she now stood, looking around.

"Cotton Candy, what's up?"

She turned around and saw Josh. Her frustration and anxiety eased somewhat upon seeing him. "I'm trying to find my cart. I was supposed to start work almost half an hour ago, and the cart wasn't where I thought it would be."

He nodded. "Depending on the time of day and how much activity is happening in different parts of the park they move the carts around. There's a big event today with some astronauts over in the Exploration Zone, so I bet it's over there."

"Real astronauts?" she asked.

"Yeah. They're here to kick off the first day of Space Camp."

"Seriously? We have a space camp here?"

He laughed. "Wow, Candy, you sure have got a lot to learn about what happens here at The Zone."

"I guess so."

"Give me a minute, and I'll find out for sure where your cart is," he said.

"Thank you," she said, relieved.

She followed him to the entrance of Kowabunga, where he reached under the podium for a walkie-talkie.

"What number is your cart?" he asked.

"Five."

He spoke into the walkie-talkie, "This is Josh over in the Splash Zone, and I'm looking for the whereabouts of cart number five. I've got a cotton candy operator here who needs to know where to go."

She could hear the answer come back, "Exploration Zone, in front of The Atomic Coaster."

"Thanks," he said before putting down the handset. "You know how to get there?" he asked.

She nodded. "If I'd gone one Zone farther I would have found it on my own, sorry."

He shrugged. "No big. Just watch out for Becca," he said, turning to deal with some players.

"Who?" she asked.

"You'll see," he said.

Shaking her head, she resumed her walk. Three minutes later she found the cart in front of one of the most popular attractions in the park.

It was called The Atomic Coaster. Huge and imposing, it dominated the landscape in the Exploration Zone. It looked like a giant atom. Three oval tracks, one vertical and two diagonal, circled around a small ball in the center. Around the entire thing was a horizontal oval track which served as part of the loading mechanism. It was beautiful, and the glistening metal soared several stories high. Tourists called it by name, speaking of it in hushed, reverent whispers as though all the mysteries of science and the universe could be discovered by riding it. Season-ticket holders brazenly called it the Atom Bomb, pretending that, after a hundred trips spinning around like a whizzing electron, it didn't scare them. The referees called it the Twirl and Hurl.

Candace walked up to the girl who was handing a cotton candy stick to a little boy. He turned and ran off, and the girl straightened to look at Candace. She was blonde and petite and, despite working with the cotton candy, had perfectly manicured nails. She glared at Candy.

"Hi, Lisa," Candace said, reading the other girl's name tag. "I'm sorry, I couldn't find the cart. I thought it would be in the Kids Zone where I was yesterday."

"They go where they're needed. If you had checked in with the manager before coming into the park, you would have known that it was here."

Candace opened her mouth to tell her that she had checked in with the manager who had said nothing about the cart's location. She changed her mind, though, and snapped her mouth shut, gritting her teeth. The other girl had the right to be miffed about getting relieved late. "I'm sorry," she said finally.

"You should be," Lisa said. She turned and left.

"That could have gone better," Candace mumbled.

"What could have gone better?" a voice asked just over her shoulder.

Candace jumped, startled, and turned to see a girl standing there wearing khaki pants and a striped khaki shirt, the outfit for Exploration Zone referees.

"I ... uh ... that is ... it was nothing."

"Oh, good. I thought Lisa was being mean to you. She can be a bit cranky."

"So I noticed," Candace said, smiling.

"Careful, she can play some dirty tricks too."

"Thanks, I'll keep that in mind."

"You're new, aren't you?"

"Yes, I'm Candace," she said holding out her hand.

"Becca," the other girl said, shaking hands.

Just watch out for Becca, Josh had said. Candace wondered what he had meant. After two seconds she already knew that she liked Becca a whole lot better than Lisa.

"What attraction do you work here?" Candace asked.

Becca inclined her head toward one of the smaller buildings. "I work at the Muffin Mansion."

At the mention of muffins, Candace's stomach growled angrily, reminding her that she had missed breakfast. She blushed. "I love muffins."

Becca shrugged. "They're good, but I prefer cotton candy."

"I'd rather have the muffins," Candace laughed.

"Hey, I've got an idea. You know if you sell food you get one free helping for yourself each day, right?"

"I remember vaguely someone saying something about that," Candace said.

"Well, it's true. Since you'd rather have a muffin, why don't I trade you my free muffin for your free cotton candy?"

Candace stood for a moment, trying to figure out what the downside could possibly be. It seemed like a fair trade, and Martha had told her she could have one cotton candy a day. "Deal," she said, shaking Becca's hand again.

"Great! I'll run over and get you a muffin. What kind would you like?"

"What kind do you have?"

"You name it, we probably have it. We have seventeen different types of muffins."

"Chocolate with chocolate chips," Candace said instantly.

"Excellent choice. I'll be right back."

Candace busied herself with the cart and had two customers before Becca returned with the muffin in a bag. Candace made her up a cone of the sticky pink sugar and handed it to her.

"Cool. Well, I gotta run. I'll see you tomorrow, Candace," Becca said, skipping off.

As she watched her go, Candace made a mental note to ask Josh why he had warned her about Becca. It made no sense. Maybe there were two Beccas. Or maybe he had confused her with someone else, like Lisa. Candace shivered.

It only took her a couple of minutes to realize that she had a perfect view of the ceremonies that were just beginning. A rudimentary stage had been set up, and she could see four astronauts sitting on it along with a couple of men in suits. In chairs on the ground were about a hundred Space Camp kids who were all wearing matching baseball caps with the NASA logo on them. From what she could tell, the camp officially started on Monday, but this event was for campers, parents, and fans of the space program.

After her lunch break, things were winding down in the Exploration Zone. Kids and parents scattered, and the guests of honor were hurried off field by referees. Twenty minutes later the zone seemed empty. The silence was eerie, and she half expected to see a tumbleweed blow through.

"Well, I guess it's just you and me, cart," she said.

As if in response, the cart gave a series of loud, high-pitched chirps. Candace jumped, startled. A low sound like a car motor began, and Candace took a step backward, suspicious and not sure that it wasn't about to explode.

Suddenly the cart lurched sideways and began to move. She yelped and dove after it, grabbing the edge of the counter and pulling. It was no use; the cart kept moving forward, and since it was bigger and heavier than she was, it began to drag her along with it.

"This is so not happening!" she shrieked. She began to flail about with her left hand, trying to find the red panic button under the counter that Martha said would summon security. All she got for her effort was two broken nails and a third that bent backward painfully.

She glanced up just as the cart reached the railroad tracks. Candace let go of the counter and stepped back. The cart lumbered slowly over the tracks as Candace heard the whistle of the train.

"Not good, not good, not good!"

Even before she had started working at The Zone, she had heard the stories about Crazy Train Guy. Rumor had it he tried to run down referees and had succeeded on more than one occasion. She glanced toward the train. Maybe it wasn't him. Maybe someone else was driving the train. She couldn't tell. Even if she had been able to clearly see the figure in the engine, she wouldn't have known because she wasn't sure what he looked like.

The cart had almost reached the other side. She couldn't lose it. Besides, the train was far enough away that it should be safe to cross. She stepped forward and instantly the train began to accelerate towards her. She jumped forward and tried to push at the cart—for the moment more terrified of something happening to it and her employer trying to take it out of her salary than concerned for her own well-being.

She could hear the train bearing down on her, the whistle piercing the air around her and making her head throb. And suddenly she was sure she was going to die. Two more jumps and she would be safe. She sprang, but her foot caught in the track and she started to fall. Twisting, she grabbed hold of the cart. She kicked her foot free and the cart dragged her off the tracks, banging her ankles hard against the pavement.

She and the cart reached the other side and the train roared past. Candace let go of the cart and fell onto her hands and knees. She twisted around to a sitting position and, raising her fist, shook it at the retreating caboose. She just wanted to sit and cry. She glanced down and saw that her ankles were bleeding. Unswayed by ankles and trains, the cart continued on its way. She scrambled to her feet and followed it, limping, until it came to a stop just inside the Game Zone.

Looking around at the kids in their baseball hats and the harried fathers trying to win stuffed animals and other prizes, she saw where everyone from the Exploration Zone had ended up.

And they all wanted cotton candy. Candy held up a hand to fend them off. She was still bleeding, and there was no way she was dispensing sticky sugary goodness in that state. Now that the cart was stable, it was seemingly easy to find the red button. And to their credit, security was there inside twenty seconds.

The lead guard took one look at her, called something in on his radio, and took charge of the situation. "This cart is temporarily closed," he told the gathering crowd.

His partner, a guy that reminded her vaguely of some TV cop, put an arm around her and moved her quickly away. "It's off to the nurse with you," he said.

Fortunately, the nurse's station wasn't that far away, and Candace soon found herself sitting on a table while a grandmotherly sort swabbed and bandaged her cuts and scrapes.

"And just what happened to you, dear?" the woman asked sympathetically.

Candace blurted out the whole story. To her relief she did so without crying, although she could feel her lower lip trembling.

"They put those new carts in last year. They're all computer controlled. When they decide business is slow and another location would be better, they move on their own. There's nothing you can do to stop them," the woman explained. "Someone should have warned you about that," she sighed. "I think it's become a bit of a prank to play on newcomers not to tell them."

"It's mean," Candace said.

"Yes. It's just lucky you weren't injured more seriously by the cart or the train." She gave Candace a cup of water and some aspirin. "Honestly, that man's a menace. I'm surprised they let him play with those two trains. Eleven cars each—that's an accident waiting to happen. I wouldn't trust him with a toy train around the Christmas tree.

41

"Now you just lie down and get some rest. I'll be back to check on you."

Candace lay down and shut her eyes. She tried not to think about what had happened, but instead thought about meeting Tamara for dinner at Rigatoni's. She was supposed to get off at nine and meet Tamara at their favorite Italian restaurant at nine fifteen. She knew it would be cutting it close, but Rigatoni's was only a couple of blocks from the park. The park was going to be open until eleven, and she was glad she wasn't stuck there that late. Then again, she was injured, so maybe that meant she could go early. Within minutes she was asleep.

"Dear, are you okay?" It was the nurse's voice, and Candace could feel her shaking her shoulder.

Candace sat up groggily. "What time is it?" she asked.

"It's almost eleven. The park's about to close. Do you feel well enough to get home by yourself, or do you need me to have someone take you home?"

Candace sat straight up. "Eleven? Tamara!"

She thanked the concerned-looking nurse before stumbling out of bed. She headed for the Locker Room, where she had stowed her purse and cell phone. Once she had them, she flipped open her cell and saw that she had six missed calls, all from Tamara.

She groaned and dialed her number.

"Hey, Tam, where are you?" Candace asked when Tamara picked up.

There was a long pause on the other end. "Well, I'll tell you where I'm *not*. I'm not eating dinner at Rigatoni's by myself because I finished eating dinner there *by myself* over an hour ago."

Candace winced. "I am so sorry. My cart went crazy and the railroad guy tried to kill me, and I've been in the infirmary."

"Are you okay?" Tamara asked.

"Yes, I think so."

"I am still mad at you," Tamara admitted.

"I'm sorry. I can't have my cell phone on me in the park, and when I got hurt they took me straight to the nurse."

"Well, I guess that's not your fault."

"Do you forgive me?"

"Yes, but I'm still mad."

"That's okay," Candace said.

"I left you messages."

"I saw, but I haven't listened to them yet. I called you first."

"Well, don't listen to the sixth one."

"Okay."

"Come to think of it, not the fourth one either."

"Okay."

"In fact, just erase them all."

"Consider it done."

"Okay."

"So, are we good?" Candace asked.

"Yeah, we're good. We can go have some ice cream," Tamara suggested.

"But I haven't had dinner yet," Candace protested.

"In that case you'll have a banana split," Tamara said.

"Fair enough."

Twenty minutes later, seated across from Tamara at Big D's ice cream shop, Candace still felt awful. They gave their orders to the waitress and Candace began to sip her water, waiting for Tamara to speak first.

"I told you this was going to happen," she finally said.

"I know," Candace answered.

"It's going to be like this all summer."

"I'm sorry."

"Then quit," Tamara said. "This is so not worth it."

"I can't."

Tamara held up a hand. "Your expenses are covered."

"Come on, Tam, you can't support me the rest of my life," Candace protested.

Tamara looked like she was about to contradict her, so Candace hurried on. "And even if you could, I wouldn't want you to. Sooner or later I'm going to have to get a job. Sure, this one has its problems, but I think I need to give it more than two days. I mean, sooner or later I'll get the hang of it."

"If this is about that guy, then just give him your phone number."

Candace could feel herself starting to get angry. Tamara didn't understand, and she didn't seem to want to try to either. "This is not about a guy. This is about my life and my future. How am I going to live in the real world if I can't handle one stupid summer job?"

Tamara studied her for a moment before saying, "You sound like your mother."

"Well, as much as I hate to admit it, she has to make sense sometimes, and this is one of those things. Please, please, please. I have to try and get through this. Can't you just try and support me *emotionally*?"

Tamara gave an exaggerated sigh, complete with a full eye roll. "Fine. I mean, if I don't who will?"

"That's what I'm talking about," Candace said. It seemed like a hugging kind of moment but the table was in the way. "VH?" Candace asked.

"VH."

VH stood for virtual hug, something they had made up when actual hugs were not possible. It was usually a phone thing, but it worked just as well now, and Candace could already feel her mood improving. She saw the waitress headed towards their table, and she picked up her spoon in anticipation. "Banana split, you are all mine."

"I want to quit," Candace wailed.

Martha patted her shoulder sympathetically. "There, there, dear. It will be all right."

"But you weren't there yesterday, Martha. It was terrible."

It had taken all of her courage to show up to work. She hadn't wanted to. She had been sore and embarrassed and more than a little frightened. She knew there was no way she could go back later, though, if she called in sick for a few days.

"I didn't have to be there to understand. All of us have a story like that one—some of us more than one. It's part of life and learning. Why, if babies stopped trying to walk the first time they fell down, the whole world would be full of people who crawled."

Candace smiled at the image. "It's so hard, though."

"Well, if it was easy, they wouldn't call it *work*, would they? You just need to stick in there. You'll get the hang of it, I promise. And who knows, you might start to like working here. I just know that whenever you start out anywhere, it's hard. And a theme park, fun as it is, is no exception."

Candace thought about it for a moment before she had to admit, "You know, Martha, you're really smart."

"Comes with age and experience," the older woman said. "Mark my words, in another week, you'll start to feel better about all this."

5

Candace had to admit that Martha was right. She had made it to the next Saturday, and things were starting to feel easier. The scratches on her ankles had healed, and she was starting to feel like she was getting the hang of the cotton candy cart. It had moved two more times on her now, and she had walked calmly beside it to the new locations without incident.

Better yet, she was beginning to appreciate the freedom that came with working a cart instead of one of the attractions. The biggest advantage was that you never knew where you would be next. After spending the previous day stuck in the Game Zone and listening to the sounds of all the midway games—loud music, popping balloons, buzzers, and the other dozen things mixed in—she was glad for a change of pace. It was with relief that she found out she'd be spending the day in the History Zone. The History Zone was broken into five sections: Ancient Egypt, Ancient Greece, Medieval Europe, Colonial America, and the Old West. Her first stop of the day was in the medieval area.

The medieval area of the History Zone was one of Candace's favorite parts of the park. The fairy-tale castle wrapped around a courtyard where vendors sold fresh apples with slices of cheese and a caramel dipping sauce, roasted turkey legs, and a variety of princess- and dragon-themed merchandise. Inside the castle you could visit Marion's Shop, which was filled with everything a little girl could want, or Prince John's Ill-Gotten Gains, where young Robin Hoods could find all the plunder they dreamed of.

The castle walls extended along a massive banquet hall that was home to King Richard's Feast. Diners ate family style at the long tables and joined King Richard in a celebration of the engagement of Robin Hood and Maid Marion. There were four seatings a day during the summer: at eleven, two, five, and eight. Candace had celebrated several of her birthdays there when she was younger.

An archway in the other castle wall led to the entrance of A Very Grimm Adventure: a dark ride through the twisted tales of the Brothers Grimm. The ride was much more frightening than any of the fairy-tale rides in the Kids Zone. As a little girl it had always scared Candace, and she had loved every minute of it.

Outside the castle walls was an area where everyone in the family could try their hand at archery. Farther on was the forest that was the home of the Merry Men. Players took a coach ride through the forest and were stopped by Robin's band of thieves who would playfully harass the passengers.

Through the month of July the medieval area was host to the Lady-in-Waiting and Squire Training Camps, which were half-day camps for kids under the age of twelve. In this training camp, boys and girls would learn all the skills they needed to be the perfect squire to a knight or lady-in-waiting to a princess. When she was ten, Candace had spent a whole week one summer in Lady-in-Waiting Training Camp.

The cart was set up close to the archery range, where players were honing their skills with bows and arrows under the tutelage of Robin Hood himself. Candace strained to get a better glimpse of the green-clad figure but couldn't tell if he was the same guy she had a crush on.

"Hey, Candace!" She turned to see Becca approaching with a small bakery bag in her hand.

"Hi, Becca," Candace called, smiling.

"Still haven't gotten your new name tag yet?" she asked.

Candace shook her head. "I've been promised that I'll get it soon."

"You better, otherwise your name will permanently be Cotton Candy."

"Great."

"Here, I brought you a muffin. It's a new kind we're trying out at the bakery, and lots of people are hooked."

"Thanks," Candace said, taking the bag and stowing it away to eat on her break. She grabbed a stick and swirled it around in the vat until she had a fluffy mound of pink to hand to Becca.

"Awesome," Becca said as she took the cotton candy.

"This is getting to be a regular thing with us," Candace noted.

Becca nodded, her eyes wide. She stepped closer to Candace and lowered her voice. "I was thinking we could make this a permanent arrangement."

Something in her voice creeped Candace out, although she wasn't sure why. When she was a kid, a traveling evangelist had done a revival at her church. She remembered the way his eyes had glittered and how much he had overwhelmed her with the sheer force of his belief. Becca had that same look in her eyes. The only word that Candace could think of to describe it was *obsession*.

"Um, sure," Candace said, holding up her hand as though to fend off an attack.

"Awwwesome," Becca said, dragging the word out. She turned and walked away, clutching her cotton candy in her fist. Candace shuddered as she watched her go.

Once Becca was out of sight, Candace returned her attention to the archery area. She was startled to discover that Robin Hood was headed her way.

She got a good look at his face. He was Orlando-Bloom handsome. With the dark hair and crackling eyes, he was more like Orlando Bloom in *Pirates of the Caribbean* than in *Lord of the Rings*. Several clusters of girls scattered throughout the area stopped to stare and point. From the way her heart started pounding, Candace knew that he was her mysterious masked stranger.

When he stopped beside her, she felt like she couldn't breathe as she stared up at him.

"Milady," he said, sweeping off his cap and giving her a courtly bow. When he straightened and put the cap on, his eyes met hers and she felt dizzy. "You are both fair and highly skilled," he said, indicating the vat of cotton candy.

"Thank you, good sir," she said, struggling to play along. She knew mascots were rigorously trained so that they could stay in character at all times. As a lowly cart operator, she lacked such training and realized she would be lucky to remember her own name. Fortunately his admiring female worshipers were standing far enough away that they couldn't hear what was being said. Candace did have the distinct, unnerving sensation of being onstage, though.

"We haven't been formally introduced. I'm Kurt," he said.

"Not Robin Hood, then?" she asked, beginning to relax a little.

He held his finger up to his lips. "Do not give away my secret identity."

"Your secret is safe with me," she said in an exaggerated whisper. "I'm Candace."

"Not Candy, then?"

"No, Candace."

"Very good, Lady Candace. It has been a pleasure, and we shall meet again soon."

With that he swept off, and his admiring fans followed from afar.

"He's something, isn't he?" Jennifer, the girl who gave Candace her breaks, said as she walked up.

"Yes," Candace said, not trusting herself to say more.

"It's hard to believe a guy like that ever went out with Lisa."

Candace felt something twist in her stomach. "Lisa, the cotton candy operator?"

"One and the same. There's no accounting for taste. Rumor has it she wants to get back together."

"What does he want?" Candace asked.

Jennifer shrugged. "He's a guy. Who can tell?"

Jennifer stepped behind the machine. "I've got it. Go take your break."

Candace remembered to grab her muffin, and she headed to the Locker Room. As soon as she was in a referee-only area, away from the eyes of the public, she tore into the muffin. It had little seeds sprinkled on the top of it and a nice lemony zest to the whole thing.

As she ate she thought about Kurt and Lisa. Lisa already didn't like her. What if she found out Candace had a crush on her Kurt? But who would tell her? Nobody at work knew. Then again, Candace figured that anyone witnessing their little meeting would have to be blind not to see that she liked him. She sighed. Any way she looked at it, Kurt was trouble. Cute, adorable trouble, but trouble nonetheless.

She finished eating and had ten minutes left to her break, so she wandered over to one of the bulletin boards and began reading.

A huge sign reminded, Don't Forget to Sign Up with Your Team for the Scavenger Hunt. Smaller notices, some handwritten and some printed, advertised everything from Roommate Wanted to TV for Sale. She turned away and saw Josh heading toward her. She waved and he trotted over.

He glanced at the bulletin board. "See anything you plan on buying?" he asked.

"Nope. Just looking. What's the whole deal with the Scavenger Hunt thing?"

"It's the big end-of-summer after-hours cast party. Everyone is divided up into teams of five. Team members are tied to each other with rope. You then run through the park following sets of clues and trying to beat the other teams. It's awesome."

It sounded kind of fun, but she wasn't sure she wanted to be tied to four other people. Plus, since she was already giving most of her summer to The Zone, she was pretty sure she didn't want to give up one of her last nights before school started back up. "I guess I'll pass," she said.

Josh laughed out loud. "Think again. It's mandatory. You *have* to go."

"If it's mandatory, then why do we have to sign up?" Candace asked.

Josh rolled his eyes. "You sign up with the people you want to be on your team."

"What if you don't have a team?"

"Then you pretty much get stuck with other people who don't have a team."

She made a face. "So, I could get stuck with someone totally random ... like that guy?" she asked, pointing to a stranger a few feet away.

Josh laughed. "Nope, he's already got a team."

"Seriously?"

"Seriously. Almost everyone does. Most of us signed up with our teams weeks ago," he said.

"So, then, I guess that means there aren't any slots on your team?" she asked, somewhat hopefully.

"Sorry. We signed up in March."

March. It figures. "What am I going to do?" she asked.

He shrugged. "You can try to find a couple of people who aren't already on a team. Otherwise you'll know in a couple of days who you're stuck with. They're posting teams on Tuesday."

"And where do I sign up if I do manage to find a team?" she asked.

"The list is in the referee cantina, behind the Exploration Zone. You been there?"

"No, but I've walked past it," she admitted.

"Well, I'm back on. Good luck," he said.

Her break was nearly over, so she hurried back to her cart and took up her position once more. While she was working, she tried to think of who she could ask that might not already be on a team. From there her thoughts drifted to Kurt. Was he on a team? He had to be. He must have plenty of friends. Maybe he was on the same team as Lisa. They could have signed up together before they broke up. If they were on a team together, what better way to rekindle the spark? Moonlight, games, competition, close proximity to each other.

Stop it! she told herself. Thinking about Kurt or Lisa—or Kurt *and* Lisa—was getting her nowhere. She needed to find team members who were as late signing up as she was. Who might be just as clueless as her?

Suddenly she got it. She just had to wait until her dinner break to act on it.

6

Candace found Sue in the last bathroom she checked. The other girl was busily cleaning up after the throngs of women who had trashed it. Candace shuddered as she remembered that it so easily could have been her cleaning bathrooms. But since Sue was the one person in The Zone who seemed to be always just a hair later than Candace, she thought she might have a winner.

Sue turned to her and gave her a bright smile. Candace noticed that her name tag said Sue and not Mary.

"Hey, Candy. Sorry, Candace," Sue said, grimacing at her slip-up.

"Hey, Sue. I see you got your name tag fixed."

"And I see you haven't."

"How is it you got yours already?"

Sue shrugged. "Lucky, I guess."

"Must be. Man, it was hard to find you. There must be like a gazillion restrooms in this place."

"Twenty-seven, but at the end of the day it might as well be a gazillion." Sue laughed. "What's up?"

"Have you signed up for the Scavenger Hunt yet?"

Sue shook her head. "I only just heard about it."

"Me too. You want to be teammates? At least that way we'll know each other."

"That would be great," Sue said, looking as relieved as Candace felt. "I was totally afraid I was going to get stuck with that crazy guy who drives the train."

"And tries to run people down? Me too. This is great, I'll go put our names down," Candace said.

"Thanks. And thanks for thinking of me."

"No problem," Candace said as she exited the restroom. She was just relieved that once again Sue was just as behind as she was. Maybe if they stuck together, the two of them could make it through the summer.

Candace headed off-field and found her way to the referee cantina. There she found a sign-up sheet tacked to the wall. She put down her name and then realized that she didn't know Sue's last name. She stood for a moment trying to decide whether to go back and ask her before finally just writing down "Sue, Janitorial" on the page. How many Sues could there be cleaning restrooms?

"Hey, are you signing up for the scavenger hunt?" a voice asked beside her.

She turned and saw a guy her age with brown hair and puppy-dog eyes.

"Yes," she said.

"Got room for one more on your team?" he asked, giving her a sheepish look. He looked like a nice-enough guy.

"Sure, you need a team?" she asked.

He nodded. "My name's Roger. I'm a cashier at The Dug Out."

"The baseball card shop in the Game Zone?" she asked.

He half nodded, half shook his head. "We carry cards for several sports: football, hockey. We also have other collectables like autographed balls, jerseys, that sort of thing. We can even take your picture and put it on a souvenir card for you, just like you were some big sports star."

"That's cool. I'm Candace. I work one of the cotton candy machines."

His eyes widened, and he leaned forward conspiratorially. "Then I don't have to tell you to watch out for Becca."

She was about to ask him why people kept saying that, but he stepped back and coughed behind his hand. "So, uh, can I be on your team?"

"Sure." She turned and wrote down his first name. "Roger what?" she asked.

"Crane," he answered.

She wrote down his last name. "Cool. Now we only have to find two more people."

He shrugged. "If you don't have a full team, they'll combine us with another team or put people who don't have a team in those slots. That happened to me last year."

She felt suddenly very sorry for him. How had he managed to be working here that long and still need to team up with a stranger? "Well, I'll catch you later, Candace," he said.

"Yeah, Roger," she answered.

He turned around, took two steps, and promptly tripped over a chair and did a swan dive onto the floor. Instantly, the room broke out in applause, and several people hastily stood up with signs on which they had scribbled scores: 8.5, 9, 7, 9.5, and one particularly loud guy held up a perfect 10.

Roger stood up slowly, blushing fiercely before heading out the door. Candace turned to a girl sitting nearby, a terrible suspicion occurring to her. "Does this happen often?" she asked.

The girl smiled. "Roger falls down or trips over something at least twice a day. I think eleven times is his personal best."

"Great," Candace said. Now she knew why Roger didn't already have a team. And come Scavenger Hunt, she was going to find herself tied to him, literally. She made a note to go home and ask her mom just how good her medical insurance was.

"It could be worse," the girl said.

"How?"

"Pete could be on your team."

"Who's Pete?"

"The guy who tries to run everyone down with the train."

"He has a name?" Candace asked, amazed.

"Other than Crazy Train Guy? Yeah, go figure. Good luck to you."

"Thanks. I think we're going to need it."

The rest of that evening her cart was parked in the Splash Zone next to the entrance to Kowabunga. It was great because she was close enough to Josh that they found time to talk when things would slack a little. The more she got to know him, the more she found she liked him. He was friendly and easy to talk to.

"Okay, so who are you crushing on?" he asked after she had sent a little girl on her way with a fistful of cotton candy.

"Excuse me? Why on earth would I tell you something like that?" she asked.

"Because I can tell you whether or not he has a girlfriend already," he said. "And because if we share and bond, it will make us like totally close."

She couldn't help it; she started laughing so hard she snorted. That got him laughing at her, and she couldn't help but laugh at that. Pretty soon her stomach ached, and she thought she was going to burst. She held up a hand.

"Stop, please, it hurts to laugh."

"Give me a name or I'll totally tickle you," he threatened.

She started laughing even harder—a shrill nervous laugh that was making people stop and stare. "Okay, I'll tell," she said, gasping. "Just don't make me laugh anymore."

"Okay, this better be good."

"You probably don't even know him," she said.

"I know everyone who works here," he assured her.

"It's Kurt, over in the History Zone."

"The mascot? Dresses up like Robin Hood and others?"

"The same," she admitted, blushing furiously.

"Well, then, it's your lucky day. I happen to know that he's available, and that he's got his eye on a certain cotton candy vendor."

She felt her heart sink. "Lisa," she said.

"No, dorko, you."

"Me?"

"Yeah, don't act all surprised. You're one of the new kids, so to speak, and you're pretty easy on the eyes."

She started blushing even harder. "You're just saying that," she accused.

"Why would I?" he asked. "I have nothing to gain. Seriously, I think he's into you. He's a nice guy too."

"Really?"

"I wouldn't steer you wrong. Only ..."

"What?"

"Well, he doesn't have a lot of ambition."

She shrugged. "Hey, I don't know what I want to do with my life yet, either."

"Yeah, but you will," he said with an easy smile. "Seriously, if you like him, you should go for it. Ask him out."

"I couldn't do that!"

"Well then, at least put yourself in the path of him asking you out."

She got butterflies in her stomach just thinking about that. He laughed at her, but it was a good-natured laugh. "That should give you something to think about, Cotton Candy."

She shook herself mentally. "So, fair's fair. Who are you crushing on?" she asked.

"No one."

"Liar."

"Nope, Scout's honor. If that changes, I'll tell you."

"Seriously, no girls you have your eye on?"

"Nope."

"You're not ... I mean, any guys you have your eye on?"

"No. If you must know, I broke up with my girlfriend a couple of months ago, and I'm just not interested in starting something new right now."

"I'm sorry. What happened?"

"Her family moved, and she didn't want to do the whole long-distance thing."

"That sucks."

"Tell me about it."

"But if you're not crushing on anyone, that's not fair. You know one of my secrets, and I have nothing on you."

"Ah, I see. With you, trust is built upon mutual blackmail."

"No, nothing like that," she said, feeling suddenly foolish.

He smiled. "No worries. I get it. You want to know one of my secrets?"

She found herself nodding.

He stepped up next to her, put his mouth close to her ear and whispered it. Startled, she looked at him.

"It's true," he said solemnly.

"Wow."

"There has now been a mutual trade of secrets so the friendship can be formally sealed. Agreed?"

"Agreed," she said. "You are a strange one, Josh."

"Don't I know it. And look, such timing. My shift is up. Here comes my replacement," he said, pointing to another surfer-looking guy walking toward them. Candace was relieved to see that next to him was Martha. Just in time too. Behind them she could see a group of kids making a beeline for her cart.

"Get out of here while you can," Martha said.

"Are you going to need help with that group?" Candace asked uncertainly.

"They don't scare me," Martha answered.

A minute later Candace and Josh were heading out of the Splash Zone. Candace started to turn right toward the Exploration Zone, but Josh put a hand on her arm.

"Let's go through the Thrill Zone."

"But it's longer that way."

"Yeah, but I want a closer look at the new coaster."

They turned left, and a minute later they were standing in front of a shiny new sign that read Glider.

Glider, the newest attraction in The Zone, was set to open the July Fourth weekend. The massive tracks swooped all around the Thrill Zone. Every so often, for the last couple of days, an empty car had gone swooshing by on a test run, causing everyone nearby to stop and stare. Candace could hardly wait to try it.

"It's going to be awesome, isn't it?" Josh asked.

"Yeah."

"Come on, let's take a closer look." Together they walked up the exit ramp.

"Hey, Greg, how's it going, Dude?" Josh asked the guy who was behind the controls of the ride.

"Josh, you're just in time. The Game Masters just left. We could use a couple of bodies on a test run."

"Really?" Candace asked. "Referee previews aren't for a couple of days."

"Yeah, well, we've already ridden it, and we could use a couple more guinea pigs," Greg said.

"We're just the guinea pigs you're looking for," Josh said.

"Then let's go."

They stepped onto the loading platform and backed into position, as though they were going on a stand-up roller coaster. Candace pulled a padded X-shaped safety bar from the left side of her body across toward her right where it locked in place. Josh did the same, and then Greg strapped two large safety belts across both of them. Now Candace was standing with her arms straight up in the air, and her heart pounding faster with each passing second.

"Who are Game Masters?" she asked Josh.

"That's what they call the engineers and designers who come up with the rides and the attractions," he said with a grin.

"Nice."

Greg stepped back and shouted, "Clear."

For a moment nothing happened. Then the platform they were standing on lifted about a foot into the air and then slowly began to tilt forward. Candace let out a little scream involuntarily. Finally, the mechanism stopped moving and she found herself parallel to the tracks, staring down at them.

"Look ahead, not down, it's cooler that way!" Greg shouted.

And then suddenly they were moving forward. Josh gave a shout, and Candace looked up as they pulled out of the station and suddenly rocketed forward.

"We're flying!" she yelled, the wind snatching the words from her lips. As they shot along with the track above and the ground below and empty sky in front of them she thought that this must be what it would feel like to be Superman. The ride banked sharply to the left and then dropped down. They both screamed as they swooped close to the ground and then pulled up and climbed high into the sky.

"This is awesome!" she heard Josh shout.

They continued on, making tight turns and dives. When they pulled back into the station and were slowly brought back to a standing position, she felt herself grinning from ear to ear. Josh was clapping and she joined him.

"That is the best ride ever," Candace panted.

"Come back during the referee preview and I'll let you go again," Greg said with a wink.

"It's good to be a ref," Josh said as they exited.

"Yeah, I think I'm starting to get the hang of it," Candace laughed. "That was so cool. I can't wait to tell Tamara about it."

As it turned out, Tamara seemed less interested in the ride than in the fact that Candace had told Josh about liking Kurt.

"Whoa, whoa, whoa! You talked to somebody at work about crushing on Kurt? You never tell anyone about your crushes except me."

"Josh made me tell. He had me laughing so hard I started snorting, and then he threatened to tickle me if I didn't spill. What's awesome, though, is he said he knew Kurt liked me too. Isn't that great?"

"Yeah. So, what are you going to do about it?"

"Josh suggested I ask Kurt out, but when I told him I couldn't do that, he said I should put myself in the way of being asked out."

"So now you're going to do what Josh says?

"Well, he is a guy and he knows Kurt, so I guess so."

Tamara had a weird look on her face that Candace hadn't seen before. She debated about asking what was up, but opted to change the topic. "So, what did you do today?"

"I hung out at the mall with Amanda and Kristen. We had our nails done," Tamara said, presenting her nails to Candace.

A pang of jealousy hit Candace. It should be her getting her nails done with Tamara. Amanda and Kristen were two of the stuck-up girls in the rich clique at school. Tamara never hung out with them.

"I thought you didn't like them," she said.

Tamara tossed her hair over her shoulder. "Well, they're not that bad once you get to know them."

Candace wouldn't know. Her family wasn't a member of the country club set, and so there was no way Amanda and Kristen would ever give her even the time of day.

"We're going to see the new Ben Stiller flick. Wanna come?"

Now Candace was really upset. "You know I can't, I'm working tomorrow."

"Are you?" Tamara asked, eyes wide with innocence.

"Yes, and you know that. What is wrong with you?"

Tamara looked down at her nails, seemingly studying their perfect, red-painted shapes. "I'm tired of your job," she said at last.

"What does that mean?"

"Your job is getting in the way of all our summer plans. I don't want you to be miserable, but I don't want you to actually *like* it. And I don't like the fact that Josh gets to hear stuff before I do."

Candace had no idea how to respond to that. It made her feel sad, and a little bit guilty, but mostly just angry. "Then maybe next summer," she said, trying to keep her voice even and emotionless, "we can get jobs together."

"Please," Tamara said, rolling her eyes. "Why would I want to work?"

7

Why would I want to work? Tamara's words still echoed around in Candace's head. She didn't have a good answer for Tamara, and she was still trying to come up with one. Of course, part of the problem was Candace still didn't have a good answer to that question for herself. Realistically, she had to work. Her dad was forcing her. Still, that didn't necessarily mean that work was evil. Lots of people did it. If work was completely evil, couldn't the whole world rebel or something?

It was because of work that she had met Josh and Kurt. That was certainly worth a measure of inconvenience and frustration. And today was the first payday, and money meant she could do stuff in her free time. So making friends and making money was certainly better than sitting in her room all day wishing she had money.

She glanced at her watch. She was fifteen minutes overdue for her morning break, and she still hadn't seen her replacement. Another five minutes passed before she saw Martha trudging toward her across the length of the Thrill Zone.

"What's up?" Candace asked when Martha came to a stop beside her.

"Megan's mom called in, and it seems she won't be working today. I'm trying to make sure everyone gets at least one break and their lunch. I'm sorry, but you'll probably have to skip your afternoon break."

"That's okay. What happened to Megan? Is she sick?"

"Love sick is more like it. She was dating a guy who worked in rides who was all wrong for her. They broke it off last night."

"Oh, that's sad."

"What's sad is that anyone with a lick of sense could have seen it coming," Martha said with a sigh. "Never date a guy you ain't willing to marry. No good can come out of that, just a lot of pain for everybody."

Wow, that's harsh, Candace thought, but she didn't say anything.

"Now go on, take your fifteen. Time's a-wasting, and it's going to be a long day," Martha said.

She sounded so tired, Candace wished there was something she could say or do to help. Since she couldn't think of anything, she scurried off to take her break. She reached the cantina at the same time as Sue.

"Aren't they supposed to post teams for Scavenger Hunt today?" Sue asked.

"I think they already have," Candace said, pointing to a crowd of people milling near one wall.

The two girls elbowed their way into the throng until they were close enough to see the list. It took a minute but they finally found their names. Sue read aloud. "Candace. Sue. Roger. Who's Pete?" she asked.

"Oh no!" Candace said. "Crazy Train Guy."

"You are kidding me!" Sue practically shouted, drawing looks from those around.

Candace had a sinking sensation in her stomach. There was only one way things could get worse. "Who is the fifth?"

"Lisa who works food carts. Do you know her?"

"Unfortunately."

The two waded back out of the throng and stood for a moment staring at each other. "I'm sorry," Candace said, finally. "I think I just pulled you into my nightmare."

Sue shrugged. "Hey, that's better than living in mine."

Candace made it back to her cart just before her fifteen minutes were up. Martha looked relieved to see her. "How'd it go?" Candace asked.

"I had eight crying kids, one mother, and a grandfather that I almost had to slap."

"Ouch. What did he do?"

"Tried to pinch me, the dirty old man."

Candace bit her lip to keep from laughing. It would seem that no matter who you were or how old you were, running a cotton candy cart opened you up to all sorts of unwanted attention.

Apparently, Martha had gotten the main rush. The cart seemed in no hurry to change locations, though, so Candace had some time to people watch.

All the coaster fanatics and thrill seekers ended up in the Thrill Zone. With nine heart-pounding attractions, four of which were major-league coasters, it had something for everyone.

For people who loved going upside down, the Spiral was a must ride. Players were loaded into cars shaped like footballs, with two seats in the front, two seats in the back, and two rows of three seats in the middle. From the loading dock, the cars moved sideways onto the track. The cars would then back up slightly, lift up into the air, and back up slightly again, before being catapulted at sixty miles an hour by a giant hand, to race along the track doing continuous 360-degree barrel rolls. Coming back into the station, an optical illusion of a giant pair of hands would catch the football car, and players would hear an announcer screaming "touchdown!" and the sound of cheering fans. Candace had been on the ride exactly twice. After the second time, Tamara had bought her an "I Survived the Spiral" jersey to replace the shirt she had thrown up on.

Having her cart parked near the exit of the ride gave Candace a great opportunity to watch and laugh at the riders coming off. Many couldn't walk straight and bounced into one handrail and then the other. Some were staggering and being held up by their friends. One guy didn't seem to have any problem at all. He walked straight and steady, but he looked out of place wearing a dark suit with a baseball cap. A guy behind him tried to walk down the ramp and ended up falling on his rump. She laughed out loud at his bewildered expression. She couldn't help but feel sorry, though, for one ten-year-old girl who was in her father's arms crying her heart out. Just because you were tall enough to ride didn't mean you should. The Spiral definitely wasn't for everyone.

Candace's thoughts drifted from the people and the roller coasters to the Scavenger Hunt. It was some kind of rotten luck that she was on the same team as the park's biggest klutz, the guy who tried to kill everybody, and the girl who had it in for her. I mean, that had to be more than random chance. She looked up toward the heavens. "Are you punishing me for something, God?"

There seemed no ready answer, but she stood like that for a moment until a high-pitched voice spoke. *God? That's not what I thought you would sound like.* She shook her head and looked down. There in front of her cart was a young girl with pigtails who was standing with a hand on her hip and staring at her like she was crazy.

"Who are you talking to?"

"God," Candace said.

"Puh-leeze. There is no such thing. My mother told me so."

"Do you believe everything your mother tells you?" Candace asked.

"Of course, she wouldn't lie to me."

Candace should have let it go. She should have stopped there and just gotten the little brat some cotton candy. She didn't though. "Does your mother tell you that you are a beautiful little girl?"

The girl tossed her head proudly. "Every day."

"Then I've got news for you. Your mother lies."

The little girl's eyes opened wide, and her bottom lip began to tremble. Then she turned and ran off.

I'm a bad, bad person. She's probably going to have self-esteem issues for the rest of her life because of me, Candace thought. *So very bad.* Candace shot up a quick prayer, *God, forgive me for that awful thing I just said. That's not the way to make friends and convert people.*

She had to try to be nicer to Lisa too. From there, though, her thoughts naturally flashed to Kurt. Josh had said that he liked her. *How on earth do I put myself in the way of being asked out? I mean, it made sense when Josh said it, but now I have no idea what that even means.*

A vibration in the cart caught her attention. Apparently there had been a long enough period of time without any activity that the cart was getting ready to move elsewhere. Candace took a step backward and let it do its thing. Less than a minute later it began to roll, and she walked alongside it. A few minutes later they arrived at their destination: the colonial area of the History Zone.

In the colonial section of the History Zone, the architecture reflected Revolutionary War-era America. A group of shops and restaurants were arrayed to give the feeling of a town. On the one end of the town was a building split in two. The left side was the printing press, a mini museum where you could learn about the history of the printed word and get a hands-on demonstration of a real old-fashioned printing press, like Benjamin Franklin might have used. On the right side was The Fine Print, a bookstore selling everything from copies of Revolutionary War pamphlets like Thomas Paine's "Common Sense" to modern fiction and nonfiction books. They also sold a large selection of writing supplies, including pens, pencils, quills, colored inks, parchment, journals, and specialty papers. Next door to that building was the pub, named Poor Richard's. The pub offered a variety of authentic dishes as well as modern fare. As they dined, patrons listened to stories from costumed characters like Ben Franklin or observed clandestine meetings between revolutionaries under the watchful eye of several Redcoats. On the other side of the pub, an antique store called Brick-a-Brack offered a wide variety of treasures for sale.

The next cluster of buildings contained several shops. The Betsy Ross Flag Shoppe specialized in anything with a flag motif and also featured a wide variety of patriotic music. Minute Men was a store where collectors could find miniatures to re-enact key events of the Revolution. Next door was Tory Towne, a shop which specialized in British merchandise both past and present and included a large variety of imported candies and choco-lates. Last was Smith's Teashoppe, which was a refined place where players could get high tea at any time of the day. Then after they had partaken, they could find themselves re-enacting the Boston Tea Party on a ship moored on a small lagoon.

The cart rolled to a stop near Paul Revere's Ride where huge numbers of kids waited in line. Within a minute Candace had sold three cones full.

Paul Revere's Ride was a giant, antique-looking carousel. Candace hadn't ridden on it in ten years, but now she had a chance to look at it closely. It was beautiful. Each horse was ornately carved with a saddle and bridle, and some sported roses, jewels, and armor. The "lead" horse carried a lantern in his teeth. The three-minute carousel ride started with an opera-tor ringing a bell and shouting, "The British are coming, the British are coming!" Tinny versions of several old songs looped over the speakers, and most recognizable was "Yankee Doodle Dandy." After a while Candace found herself humming along. She also found herself keeping a sharp eye out for a certain handsome masked stranger.

And like magic, he appeared. Candace blinked, thinking for a moment he was a figment of her imagination. But there he was, walking toward her, larger than life.

He stopped in front of her and just stared at her for a moment, a little smile twisting the corners of his mouth.

"Can I help you?" she blurted out.

"You sure can," he said. "I'm looking for a young lady to take out to dinner tonight, and I was wondering if you knew of any young ladies who were free for dinner and not adverse to being seen in public with the likes of me?"

Over the sudden pounding of her heart, Candace thought she had just heard him ask her out. *Be cool, be cool,* she told herself. *Think of something clever.*

"That's me." *Smooth, Candace, real smooth.*

"Wonderful. What time are you available?"

"I get off at five, but I'd like to go home and change," she said, pointing to her pink-striped blouse.

"Shall I pick you up at six thirty then?"

She nodded. From somewhere he produced a pen and paper and she wrote down her address and phone number.

"Until tonight then," he said, giving her a bow.

"Yes," she said, breathlessly.

He moved on then, walking past her cart. It was then that she noticed that her cart was parked in the middle of the road on which he had been walking. *She was literally in his path!* She laughed out loud and patted the cotton candy cart. "You did just fine, thank you."

8

Candace couldn't focus the rest of the morning. When Martha finally relieved her for lunch, an hour late, she raced toward the Splash Zone. Josh saw her coming from a ways off and waved to her.

"Guess what?" she said.

He looked at her closely, squinting. "Well, either you just got named Referee of the Month or Kurt asked you out."

"Kurt. Me. Asked."

"Awesome! And when is the happy date?"

"Tonight!" she squealed.

"Dude doesn't waste time. Where are you going?"

"I don't know. He didn't say. He's picking me up at my house at six thirty."

"Sweet. You'll have to tell me all about it tomorrow."

"I don't work Wednesdays," Candace said.

"Then Thursday. Or you can email me. ZonerJosh at yahoo dot com."

"Got it," she said. "I'm so nervous."

"Just be yourself—you know, the sweet Cotton Candy we've all come to know and love."

She rolled her eyes. "Come on, Josh. He barely knows me. *You* barely know me. How do you even know I'm sweet?"

"Because it's obvious. Duh. Besides, we swapped secrets. You can tell a lot about a person when you do that."

"Like what?" she asked.

"Like you're trustworthy. If you weren't, the whole park would know my secret by now."

She blushed. "It's not my secret to tell."

"Exactly. And that tells me that you are a good, kind person."

"You are something else, Josh."

"Thank you, I take that as a compliment. Now you better take off. I see a whole group of kids coming my way, and I can already tell you that half of them aren't going to pass the height requirement. It could get ugly."

"Good luck," she said, before heading off.

She found she was too excited to eat her lunch, so she returned to her cart early. Martha looked at her in surprise. "You're back early."

"Nothing better to do at the moment," Candace confessed.

"You sure? There won't be an afternoon break."

"That's okay. I'm good. Just make sure someone relieves me at five."

Martha looked at her closely. "Got somewhere to be tonight?"

"I have a date," Candace said, blushing.

Martha smiled. "Have fun, dear. I'll make sure you get off in time." Martha left without warning Candace about not dating guys she wouldn't want to marry. Candace was relieved. That would have been a lot of pressure to put on a first date.

She thought five o'clock would never come, but it finally did, bringing Martha with it. "I brought you your check to save you some time," Martha said, handing Candace an envelope with her name on it.

"Great!" Candace said, eagerly tearing open the envelope.

She pulled out the check. It had her name, Candace Thompson, on it. At least the accounting department got her name right! She looked at the amount. "Three hundred and ninety-six dollars. That's it? Where did all my money go?"

Martha laughed. "Candace, the real world. The real world, Candace," she said as though making introductions. "Read your check stub, and it will show you where all your money went."

Candace did as Martha instructed. "Why does the government need so much of my money?" she asked, bewildered. "They didn't earn it, I did. Oh man, that stinks."

"Tell me about it. Now you better go on and get out of here so you'll be ready for your date."

"Thanks," Candace said, cheering up at the thought. "I'll see you later."

As soon as Candace got her purse out of the Locker Room, she tried calling Tamara's cell. "Come on, Tam, pick up."

The phone rang several times before going to her voicemail.

"Tam, guess what? The cute guy in the Zorro costume asked me out! We're going out tonight. Call and help me figure out what to wear." She slipped the phone and the check into her purse and headed for the car.

Once home, she raced up the stairs and peeled off her uniform, then threw open her closet doors and stared in dismay at her wardrobe. She picked up her phone and called Tamara again. "Please, Tam. I've got an hour and I don't know what to wear. Call soon."

She stood in front of the closet touching first one thing and then another. Finally she threw herself down on her bed and grabbed her stuffed bear.

"Mr. Huggles, what am I going to wear?" she asked him. He stared back at her with his warm, supportive eyes but seemed to have nothing to say on the matter. He was much better at protecting her from monsters than helping her deal with boys. She hadn't even thought to ask Kurt where they were going, so she had no idea how casual or how fancy to dress up.

Tamara would know. Tamara could tell her exactly what to wear, if only she would call. Candace grabbed her phone and flipped it open, just to make sure she didn't have the phone on vibrate. Nope. It wasn't, and there were no voice or text messages for her. There was no help for it; she had no way of knowing when Tamara was going to call.

She heard the front door open and the click of her mom's heels in the entryway. She got up and crossed to her door. "Mom, could you come help me, please?"

There was a pause from downstairs and then she heard her mom's steps on the stairs. "Is everything okay?"

"Yes. And no."

Her mom appeared, looking concerned. "Well, what is it?"

Candace sat down on her bed as her mom came into the room. "I've got a date with a cute guy from work tonight and I can't decide what to wear."

"Who is this boy and what is he like?" her mom asked, going into her best grilling mode.

"Mom, please. I'll tell you all about him later, but right now I need your help. He's going to be here to pick me up in less than an hour."

Her mom sighed and kicked her shoes off. "Okay, where are you going?"

"I don't know. That's part of the problem. Dinner, I think, but I don't know where."

"You're not giving me a lot to work with here."

"I know, that's why I need help," Candace said, letting herself fall backwards until she was sprawled across the bed.

Her mom walked over to the closet. "This guy, how tall is he?"

"At least six feet."

"Okay, so you can get by with heels and not end up taller than him. Most guys say they don't have a problem with that, but most of them are lying. What kind of job does he have at the park?"

"He's one of the costumed characters. Mostly he's dressed up like the Lone Ranger or Zorro or Robin Hood. He's really good at it too, he can totally stay in character."

"Okay, so he's got a bit of a taste for the theatrical. You'll want a little drama and contrast in what you wear, then."

Candace sat up and stared at her mom. She would never have thought of these things on her own. She didn't think Tamara would have, either.

"Where's that black skirt we got you last year? You know, the one you never wear?"

"You mean, the skirt I got to wear to cousin Alice's funeral?"

"Yes, that one."

"All the way to the left. But I don't think—"

"Found it," her mother interrupted.

She tossed the skirt and Candace caught it. Next her mother bent over and inspected her shoes. "These are all you have?" she asked after a minute.

"Yes," Candace said, feeling inexplicably embarrassed. Her mother turned and looked at her for a moment.

"Put the skirt on. I'll be right back."

Her mom headed toward her bedroom, and Candace slipped on the skirt. It was straight and form fitting. It was also shorter than Candace remembered, ending several inches above her knees. In a minute her mother returned, arms full.

"Try on this," she instructed, handing Candace a teal shirt.

It took Candace a minute to figure out how to put it on. It turned out the shirt was a wrap-around. Once it was on she was surprised to find that it fit really well. She was also surprised that it was lower cut than anything she owned.

"And these," her mom said, handing her a pair of her shoes. "We wear the same size, so they should fit."

They were black strappy sandals with two-inch heels. Candace slipped them on and was surprised at how comfortable they were. Her mom nodded. "Those are great shoes. They look great and you can stand all night in them if you have to. Now, pull your hair back in a small black barrette, and let's see what that looks like."

Candace did as her mother said and then stared at herself in her full-length mirror. Her mom came to stand beside her and nodded as though satisfied.

"Well?" she asked.

"Wow," was all Candace could say.

"You do clean up very nicely. What's nice about this look is you won't be out of place if he takes you somewhere upscale. If he takes you somewhere more casual, you'll be comfortable and he'll be priding himself on having the most dazzling girl in the place."

"Thanks, Mom."

She kissed Candace on the cheek. "Don't say I never did anything for you. Don't forget some lipstick."

"I won't."

"And don't let him paw at you. Just because you look stunning isn't an excuse for him to be ill-mannered."

"I'll remember that," Candace said, blushing at the thought.

"Take your cell phone. If you need anything, or he gets weird or tries anything, or even if he's just boring you to death, you call and we'll come get you."

Candace turned and hugged her mom. Sometimes she got frustrated because she felt like her parents were harder on her than they should be, but she could always count on them to come through when she needed them. "I will," she promised.

"Okay. Then knock him dead."

Her phone rang. Candace picked it up as her mom left the room. "Hello?"

"Hey, it's Tam."

"Tamara! I'm going on a date."

"So I heard. You need help with clothes?"

"Not anymore. My mom totally came through. You should see me; I look hot."

"Cool. Send me a picture. Since you're good, I gotta run. Having dinner with the folks tonight."

"Oh, okay."

"Don't forget the picture."

"I won't."

As soon as they hung up, Candace turned her phone around and took a picture of herself. For once she actually managed to take a decent one. She usually cut off half her face when she tried. She sent it to Tamara, hoping she would love the look as much as Candace did.

She stared again at herself in the mirror. "I can't believe I never realized how cute this skirt is," she said, twirling.

After fixing her makeup and transferring her things to her small black purse that she usually took to church, she headed downstairs to wait. Her father looked up from his magazine, eyes narrowed.

"What do you think, Daddy?" she asked.

"Turn."

She did a slow twirl. "Well?"

"Very nice."

"You think he'll like it?"

"I'll think he's a blind fool if he doesn't. I also think I'll slap him walleyed if he stares."

"Daddy, you wouldn't!"

"Care to test that theory?"

"No, just be nice, please."

"I'm always nice," he said. He reached into his pocket and dug out his wallet. "I know you haven't had a chance to cash your paycheck yet, and I don't want you going out with some strange guy without money. Just in case." He pulled several bills out of his wallet. "This is a loan only. I expect to be paid back."

She took the money from him and slipped it into her purse. "I will," she promised.

"Now be careful, and call if you need us."

"I will."

At exactly six thirty the doorbell rang, and Candace ran to get it. Kurt stood there wearing khaki Dockers and a black button-down shirt. His eyes widened when he saw her, and she couldn't help but smile like an idiot.

"Wow, you look great," he said.

"Thank you," she answered. "You look very nice too."

His eyes widened more, and she felt a hand descend on her shoulder. She stiffened slightly.

"Young man, make sure she's home before midnight," her father said.

"Yes, sir."

"Dad, this is Kurt. Kurt this is my father, Mr. Thompson." She didn't know what else to say. She turned and kissed her father on the cheek. "See you later, Dad."

He didn't look at her but continued to stare at Kurt in a way that made the hair on the back of her neck stand up. Her dad could be scary when he wanted to.

A minute later she was in Kurt's car, and they were pulling away from the house. When they had turned off her street, Kurt seemed to relax.

"What does your father do for a living?" he asked.

"He's an attorney," Candace said.

"I believe it."

"So, where are we going?" Candace asked.

"This little Italian restaurant called Rigatoni's. I hear they have great food. Have you ever been there?"

"Once or twice," Candace said with a smile. *Once or twice a month was more like it.* She settled back into her seat. For some reason it made her more relaxed to think that she would at least have the home-court advantage, so to speak. It meant she could focus the majority of her attention on Kurt and on making sure she didn't say something lame.

9

"Welcome back, Candace," the waiter said with a smile.

"Thank you, Anton."

"Do you know what you'd like?"

Of course she knew what she was going to order, but Kurt had never been there before. "I think we're going to need a couple of minutes," she said.

"Very well. I'll be back with your bread."

Kurt was looking at her with raised eyebrows. "Once or twice?"

She shrugged. "It's one of my favorite restaurants."

"Then I guess I picked well," he said.

"Yes, you did." She smiled.

When Anton returned, Candace ordered the chicken fettuccine alfredo, and Kurt ordered the classic spaghetti with meat sauce. When the waiter had departed, Kurt leaned closer.

"So, tell me about yourself."

"Well, I'm an only child. My dad's a lawyer. My mom's an environmental activist. I'm working as a cotton candy operator, as you know, and it is my first job ever. Next year I'm going to be a senior, and I'm really looking forward to that. I like roller coasters, cookie dough ice cream, Italian food—obviously—and movies."

"So then, this would be a perfect date if after dinner we went to a movie where we ate cookie dough ice cream and then took a quick spin on one of the rides in the Thrill Zone?"

She laughed. "Maybe all but the last part. It's funny. Working at The Zone makes me less inclined to spend my downtime there."

He smiled. "I get that. I used to spend every weekend at that place until I started working there. Now unless I'm there to work, I'm not there."

"I guess that happens to everyone."

"Oh, you'd be surprised. Quite a lot of refs spend their free time there too. It's like some weird obsession with them. Fans first, employees second. I feel kind of sorry for them."

"I don't know where they find the time," Candace said. "I've had barely any free time since I started working there. There's no way I could keep it up year round with school and everything."

He nodded.

"So, what about you? Where do you go to high school?" she asked.

"I don't."

Her eyes widened. "So, you're in college?"

"Nope. No school for me. I actually dropped out of high school the middle of last year."

She laughed, but quickly stopped when he didn't join her. "Oh, you're serious?"

He nodded. "I couldn't stand school so I figured, why bother?"

"Oh." Candace wasn't sure what to say next. Fortunately, the appearance of some familiar faces kept her from having to come up with something. She waved and Kurt turned to look. Coming through the door were Tamara and her parents. The three of them looked shocked and waved back. They were quickly escorted to a table but Tamara broke off from her parents. Candace stood up quickly and hugged her. She wished she could thank her for saving her from further embarrassing herself, but that would have to come later.

"Kurt, this is my best friend, Tamara. Tamara, this is Kurt," Candace said, making the introductions.

"How do you do?" Kurt asked, shaking her hand.

"Well, thank you," Tamara said. "Well, don't let me interrupt. I can see my parents are waiting for me."

She turned away from Kurt and whispered "Call me later" to Candace before joining her parents.

"Wow, how weird was that?" Candace asked.

"Pretty strange," Kurt admitted. "So, where were we?"

"You were telling me how you came to be Robin Hood," she said, making something up to avoid talking about school.

"Now, that's a funny story," he said, his eyes lighting up.

As he began telling her the story, she couldn't help but think about what she had just found out. How on earth could he be a high-school dropout? She didn't have any overly ambitious plans for herself, but she knew that she was going to college, and she was certainly going to graduate from high school. She always figured that once she got to college she would have the opportunity to figure out what she wanted to do with her life. She wondered what Kurt could possibly have in mind for his. She shook her head, trying not to think about it.

Their food arrived, and they both ate hungrily, making small talk. Afterward Candace got up to use the restroom. A moment later Tamara joined her. "He is even better looking out of his costume," her friend said.

"He is handsome, isn't he?" Candace asked wistfully.

"Sounds like he's pretty funny too. I've heard you laughing a lot."

"Have I?" Candace asked, surprised.

"Girl, what is wrong with you? You're acting all weird."

"What if he's not perfect?"

"What guy is?" Tamara asked.

"Yeah, I guess."

"So, what's wrong with him?"

"He dropped out of high school."

Even Tamara seemed slightly taken aback. "To do what?" she asked finally.

"I don't know. I don't think he knows."

"Well, some guys just take a little longer to figure out what they want from life. It's probably just a phase. Sooner or later he'll figure it all out."

"You think?"

"Sure. He'll surprise everybody and decide to become a brain surgeon or something."

"Okay. From slacker to surgeon. That's a bit of a leap, even for you."

"Call me a hopeless romantic. Everything else cool?"

"Yeah, he's very sweet."

"Great, then get back out there and strut your stuff."

"Thanks."

"By the way, your mom? Great taste."

"Who knew?" Candace said.

"I know. I might have to call her next time I have a big date."

Candace laughed. "Come on, Tam, you've got designers willing to help you out with that."

"True. Call me later."

"Will do."

When Candace returned to the table, Kurt was staring at the bill and frowning. "Can I help pay?" Candace asked timidly, worried that the bill might be higher than he had expected.

"No, I've taken care of it," he said, snapping the bill folder shut and placing it on the table. "Shall we go get some ice cream?"

They went next door to get Baskin-Robbins, and then sat outside to eat their cones. It was a nice night—not too warm—and the moon was out and shining brightly. Fortunately the ice cream was hard so that none of it dripped onto her outfit.

Afterward he drove her home and walked her up to her door. "I had a nice time," she told him, standing on the porch and holding her house key. "Thank you."

"Did you have a nice enough time to want to do this again?" he asked.

"I would like that a lot," she said.

"Great. I'll see you at work tomorrow?"

"You bet," she answered.

He was standing very close to her, and she was looking up into his gorgeous eyes. Suddenly he bent down and kissed her gently on the lips. It lasted for only a second, and then he was gone and halfway to his car. She leaned against the door for support and touched her hand to her lips. It had been so sudden that she had a hard time believing it had actually happened.

She went inside. She poked her head into her parents' bed-room and said goodnight before retreating to her own room. She changed into her pajamas and then called Tamara.

"So did he kiss you?" Tamara asked by way of greeting.

"Yes."

"Tell."

"It was real quick. He kissed me soft on the lips and then ran to his car."

Tamara laughed. "He was probably worried that your dad was taking aim at him with a shotgun."

"Please."

"Have you met your father? He can be scary."

"I guess. So are we still on for tomorrow?"

"You better believe it. I'm picking you up at eight, and we're going to tear up the town."

"Sounds like a plan. I better get some sleep then. See you in the morning."

"Night."

She remembered that Josh wanted to hear about her eve-ning, so she sat down at her computer. She started a new email message and typed in the address: ZonerJosh@yahoo.com. In the subject line she typed Date with Kurt.

Josh, things went really well tonight. He took me to Riga-toni's. It was really funny because my best friend Tamara was there eating with her parents. It's the first time she's seen Kurt out of costume. Actually, it was the first time I've seen Kurt out of costume. I took your advice and tried to just be myself. We had lots of fun, and he even kissed me good night. The kiss was really quick (I think he was worried that my father might be watching through the window) but it was awesome.

More later. Candace

P.S. Did you know he dropped out of high school? That's a little weird. Oh well. Nobody's perfect. TTFN.

Candace began to get ready for bed. A couple of minutes later her email alert sounded. She hurried over to her computer and saw that Josh had emailed her back.

Candy, glad things went well. Funny that your friend was at the restaurant. Kurt emailed me a while ago and said how hot you looked. Send a pic if you have it. Josh

Candace grabbed her phone and sent the picture she had taken to his email address. Then she replied to his message.

Josh, I just sent the picture. Let me know if you get it. It's a little weird, both of us talking to you. You're not telling him what I'm saying are you? Candy

A minute later he replied.

Got your pic. He didn't do you justice. Wow! And don't worry. I'm on your side. Sure, you're both my friends, but I like you best. :)

It was nearly one a.m. by the time she and Josh said good night. Candace fell into bed and whispered "Thank you, God" before she fell asleep.

The next morning when Tamara picked her up at eight, Candace tumbled into her car yawning.

"Couldn't sleep?" Tamara asked.

"I was up late emailing with Josh."

"Oh," Tamara said, her voice suddenly frosty.

Candace wasn't in the mood to deal with that so she let it go. "That was cool last night when you showed up at the same restaurant."

"It was pretty funny," Tamara said, her voice relaxing. "You know, my parents kept suggesting that we ask you and Kurt to join us."

"Oh my gosh! Are you serious?"

"Totally. I finally said, 'What part of *date* don't you understand?'"

"I bet that went over well."

"My mom was ticked, but my dad thought it was hilarious. I think he thought we had interrupted enough. That's why he paid for your dinner."

"He what?" Candace asked, suddenly alert.

Tamara glanced at her, looking puzzled. "Kurt didn't mention that?"

"It must have slipped his mind," Candace said grimly. "I went to use the restroom, and when I got back he was staring at the bill with a weird look on his face. I was afraid it was more expensive than he had thought, and I volunteered to help, but he said that he'd already taken care of it."

"Okay, that's odd. My dad paid for it and had Anton put a note to that effect in the bill holder."

"I wonder why Kurt didn't say anything?" Candace asked. It seemed really weird to her.

Tamara shrugged, clearly not as worried about it. "Maybe it made him uncomfortable or embarrassed, or he just didn't know what to say."

"Yeah, I guess."

"He was probably planning to impress you by paying for your dinner, and Dad ruined his plans. Guys are weird. Sometimes they get all proud about the strangest things."

It made sense, but Candace still didn't like it.

After eating breakfast at Denny's, they headed for the mall where they walked around and did some serious window shopping. Next they headed for the movie theater where Candace was determined to catch up on the movies that she wanted to see.

It was a good day mostly, but every time Candace brought up work or anyone there, Tamara got all weird acting. Candace was getting tired of it, but didn't know what to say or even how to bring it up. So she kept her mouth shut.

"Wanna go for coffee?" Tamara asked as they left the last feature.

Candace glanced at her watch. It was already nine o'clock. "I better not. I've gotta be to work early."

"Oh, that," Tamara said shortly, a note of disdain in her voice.

"Are you going to come by the park tomorrow?" Candace asked.

"Maybe."

"I'd love for you to meet Josh and some of the others."

"We'll see. I'm not sure I'll be in the mood to meet new people."

"Well, then just come by and say hi. Work that season ticket."

"We'll see."

They had reached Candace's house, and she got out of the car slowly. "Well, see you tomorrow, hopefully."

"Yeah, night," Tamara said before driving away.

Candace stood and watched her go. She couldn't help but feel like she was losing Tamara, but she wasn't sure why or what she could do to stop it.

Candace didn't sleep well, plagued by worry over Tamara and anxiety over going back to work and seeing Kurt. The stress of both was too much to let her sleep more than a few fitful bursts.

The next morning she was moving slowly. She was so exhausted she barely made it to work on time. When she got there, Martha was waiting for her with arms crossed and a stern look on her face. *Uh-oh*, Candace thought. She had no idea what for, but she could tell she was in trouble.

10

"What is it?" Candace asked Martha.

"You signed up to work overtime yesterday, and you didn't show up."

For a horrible moment she felt her heart plunge, but a moment later it rallied. "I didn't sign up to work overtime," she protested.

Martha raised an eyebrow. "Then do you care to explain how your name got on the list?"

"I don't know how my name got on the list, but I didn't put it there. I can barely handle working forty hours a week. Why on earth would I sign up for more?"

"That's what I would have thought, but apparently you did."

"Show me," Candace demanded. And in that moment she realized that she was more like her father than she would ever have dreamed. If they wanted to declare her guilty, they were going to have to prove it beyond a reasonable doubt.

Martha led the way through the Locker Room. There, near the entrance, was a wall with sign-up sheets on it. Under *Wednesday*, someone had written her name. Only they had misspelled her last name, leaving off the *p* in Thompson.

"That's not my handwriting, and whoever wrote it didn't even spell my name correctly," Candace said, anger flooding her. Until that moment she had thought there must have been a genuine mistake, that somebody with a similar name had signed up, and people had misread it. Now she knew that someone had deliberately done this to her, and she had a pretty good idea who.

"Do you know who might have done this?" Martha asked, her conviction wavering.

"Lisa. Becca warned me that she played tricks on people, and she hates me. Tuesday night when I was on my date, it was with her ex-boyfriend."

Comprehension dawned in Martha's eyes. Slowly she began to nod.

"I'm going to get her," Candace vowed.

Martha put a hand up. "You don't want to do that. If you start trading revenge with her, it's going to get ugly. It's going to get out of control, and someone could get really hurt. Leave it to me. There are proper ways to deal with these things."

"What are you going to do to her?" Candace seethed.

"That's my problem, not yours. I'm sorry that this happened to you."

"I'm not in trouble, right?" Candace asked, still angry at being set up and unjustly accused.

"No, you're not. Now go to work."

Candace's spirits improved slightly when she discovered the cart was in the History Zone but then plummeted again when she learned it was in the Ancient Egypt area. To the best of her knowledge, Kurt never worked in that part. Although she could imagine him dressed up like a pharaoh.

She trudged toward her area, wondering what exactly Martha would do to Lisa and hoping it included firing her. Otherwise, Candace was pretty sure she would kill Lisa when they were tied together for the Scavenger Hunt. Either that or, through his klutziness, Roger would kill all of them. Of course, Pete might find a way to do that anyway.

She passed through the colonial area and looked quickly around but didn't see Kurt anywhere. She took the bridge over the river and ended up on the island that encompassed Ancient Egypt. As she stared around looking for her cart, she felt again the same awe as when she had first seen the island as a child.

Egypt was overwhelming with its three pyramids stretching toward the sky. The largest one was in the center. Candace remembered hearing somewhere that, like the pyramids in the real Egypt, they were supposed to align with each other, just like the stars in Orion's belt in the night sky. Around the three pyramids there was a bazaar with permanent tents and carts offering food and merchandise. It was always a busy, noisy place with the merchants hawking their wares loudly.

The Great Pyramid was a popular, fast-moving ride where riders pretended to be amateur archaeologists trying to outwit and outmaneuver traps set by the ancient pharaohs. Players who shot a mummy with an old-fashioned toy pistol anchored to the dash of the jeep won a piece of the pharaoh's treasure, usually a shiny plastic stone or piece of jewelry or a cup.

The pyramid to the right of The Great Pyramid contained a restaurant called King Tut's, which boasted "A buffet fit for a pharaoh." The walls were decorated with all manner of hieroglyphs, and diners could request a translation card to help them read the various writings.

The third pyramid was called the Tomb of the Pharaohs. The entire pyramid was one gigantic maze filled with wall paintings and educational displays. Just to keep players from getting too complacent, the walls were movable, and the entire pattern of the maze would change every month.

Candace hated mazes. She didn't have the world's greatest sense of direction, but that didn't entirely explain her fear and dread of them. No, it was that she hated feeling trapped, and she had spent enough time in a house of mirrors at a carnival when she was eight to never want to feel trapped or disoriented again. Ever. She had, in fact, never been inside the Tomb of the Pharaohs for just that reason.

Even though Ancient Egypt had the one attraction in the park she would never, ever see, it also had one of her favorites. In the Nile River around Egypt, there was a boat ride called Queen of the Nile. Two elaborate barges that resembled ancient royal Egyptian vessels circled the river. Both ships were magnificent, and they differed slightly from one another. The larger of the two was called *The Spirit of Cleopatra*, and the smaller was called *The African Queen* as an homage to the Humphrey Bogart and Katharine Hepburn movie.

It took her several minutes, but she found her cart in a remote corner close to the river. Becca, it seemed, had no trouble finding the cart, because ten minutes later she arrived, carrying her usual muffin bag.

"I brought you the same one you've been having."

"Thanks, they're really good."

"Lots of people like them. Even Dr. Scott, the president of the park, is hooked on them."

"The president spends time in the park?" Candace asked, surprised.

"Sure, he walks through at least twice a week. You've probably seen him. He's usually wearing a dark suit with some sort of red tie and a baseball cap."

"Oh yeah, I've seen that guy," Candace said. "That's the president?"

"Yup. He likes to make sure everything is running smoothly and see what's going on for himself. That's why he spends so much time in the park. Personally, though, I just think he likes it better than being cooped up in his office."

Candace laughed at that. "You could be right. Well, I better get you your cotton candy so you can get back to the Muffin Mansion."

"Thank you," Becca said.

The swap made, Becca waved and headed off, weaving between the throngs of people beginning to fill the area. It wasn't long before several in the throngs had patronized Candace's cart. She looked up at one point, and it seemed as though a sea of cotton candy was floating above the heads of the crowd.

She started laughing, and for the first time since arriving at work, she felt her mood truly lighten. With perfect timing, Kurt appeared, looking incredibly out of place in his green tunic and leggings.

"I didn't realize that Robin Hood plundered the rich as far away as Egypt," she said, amusing herself.

"Not usually, but I do make exceptions, especially when there are lovely damsels to rescue," he said.

"Am I in need of rescuing then?" she asked.

He moved in closer. Somehow, when he was in the costume, he seemed larger than life and more handsome than ever. "I think you are," he said, his voice a low purr.

"And from what—"

She didn't get to complete her question because he took her in his arms and kissed her. Unlike the kiss on her doorstep, this one was bold, strong, and seemed to last forever. When he let her go, she gave a little sigh of disappointment.

"There, I have rescued you from your ordinary day," he said, a look of triumph on his face.

"You sure have," she murmured.

"Eeeewwww." She turned and saw a chorus of five-year-olds making faces. She laughed and felt herself turn bright red.

"And now that I have rescued you, I am off to rob from the rich." He swept away, leaving her to deal with the face-making children who thought that—gross as the display had been—it was not enough to distract them from their desire for sugary goodness.

By the time Candace had handed out cones to all of them, her replacement had arrived. She didn't say a word, but handed Candace a slip of paper. Candace unfolded it and saw that it was a note to report to the nurse's office. She looked up questioningly at the girl who had brought it, but the new girl was already busying herself with the cart.

Candace shrugged and headed off, grabbing her muffin which she ate on the way. Thanks to her first experience with the cart running away from her, she knew where to go. The same matronly nurse who had helped her then was there now. Candace showed her the note, and the woman handed her a cup with a label on it.

"What's this for?" Candace asked.

"Random drug testing. Today we picked random last names from the last third of the alphabet."

"Drug testing? Seriously?" Candace asked.

"Yes, it's in your employment agreement, dear, if you want to read it."

"No, that's okay. What do I do with the cup, though?"

For just a moment she thought the nurse was going to start laughing. She only smirked, though, before saying, "The drug test is a urine test. I'll need you to go fill that. The women's room is down the hall on your right."

"Eew," Candace said before she could stop herself.

At that, the nurse did start laughing. "You'll be fine."

Ten minutes later Candace was finished and had put the cup in the appropriate box in the bathroom. She approached the nurse. "Is there anything else?" she asked.

"No, that's it. Results will be available in a day or two and are sent to your supervisor. You can go back to work now."

Candace left and wondered if the whole trip to the nurse was supposed to count as her break or if she was now free to take it. After a minute's debate she decided it would be best to return to the cart. There had been enough craziness already without her getting accused of going AWOL on a break.

Back at the cart things were quiet. The sea of cotton candy was slowly being replaced by a sea of balloons. Candace watched them as they moved this way and that in the breeze and in response to the movements of their owners. Some drifted along slowly while others moved at a good speed. She wondered idly what it would be like to be one of those balloons, tossed by the changes in air currents.

The girl who had relieved her must have left a pen behind. Candace spread out a couple of napkins and began to doodle on them to take her mind off everything else. Pretty soon one of the doodles started to resemble a ride. She stared at it, thinking hard, before drawing some more.

A different girl came to relieve her for lunch, so Candace took the pen with her. She stopped by The Dug Out, and Roger gave her a couple of sheets of paper that she could draw on. She thanked him and found a quiet bench where she could continue drawing.

Art was one of the school classes she had always liked. She didn't consider herself an artist, but she could draw basic shapes pretty well. She continued sketching as her ride came to life. At the top she wrote the name: *The Balloon Races*.

"What are you drawing?" Josh asked, sitting down on the bench next to her.

"It's nothing," she said, suddenly embarrassed and not sure why.

"Come on, let me see. That's a ride, isn't it?"

"Yeah."

"The Balloon Races. Cool name."

"It's an indoor ride. You get into a basket that looks like the basket of a hot-air balloon, and then you rise into the air and soar over cityscapes and parklands. There are these levers that can control just how high you go. You can even turn this knob to make yourself go faster."

"You'd have to space the cars out to account for people going slower or faster."

"Yeah, but it's doable."

"This is really cool," he said. "Are you going to enter it into the contest?"

"What contest?" she asked.

"The scholarship contest. It's open to high school employees of The Zone. You enter your ride ideas, and the winning one gets built in Zone World. The winner gets a full scholarship to Florida Coast University for a degree in design or engineering or something related."

"No, I haven't heard of it," Candace said.

"You should totally enter. This is awesome!"

"No. This is a daydream, not much more than a doodle. I wouldn't stand a chance. And even if I did, I'm not going to Florida. I'm going to Cal State."

"Well, then, what are you going to do with it?" he asked.

She shrugged. "Probably toss it."

"Can I have it then? It's cool."

"If you want it," she said.

"I do. Here, sign the bottom for me."

She did, feeling a little strange.

"Awesome. Now I'm in possession of a certified Cotton Candy original."

She laughed. "The first and last piece in her promising art career."

"Then I'm even more honored."

She stood. "Good. You're honored, and I'm almost late. I'll see you later."

As she walked back toward Egypt, she thought about what he had said about the scholarship competition and found herself wishing that she actually had taken some real art classes. Maybe then she'd have something worth entering.

11

Saturday when Candace arrived at work, it wasn't Martha, but another supervisor, Ron, who was waiting for her with crossed arms. "You've got to be kidding me," Candace said. "What has Lisa signed me up for now?"

"I can assure you that Lisa has nothing to do with this," Ron said. "Grab your stuff and go home."

"What? Why?" Candace asked, startled.

"You failed your drug test."

"I what?" Candace asked, confused.

"You failed. As in, the screening showed traces of illegal substances in your system."

"No, it couldn't. I mean, how could it? I don't do drugs."

"You might want to keep your voice down," Ron said. "No need to share with everyone." He grabbed her by the elbow and started maneuvering her toward the door.

She yanked her arm free. "Let go of me!" she shouted. "You have no right to grab me like that. I do not do drugs. The test is wrong!"

Ron was getting red in the face. It was clear that he was trying to get her to leave—and to leave quietly. That wasn't going to happen. Dozens of other refs who were just getting to work or just leaving were now staring at both of them. On the other side of the room she saw someone take off running. *They're going to get security!* she thought, panic setting in hard.

"This is the second time this week I've been falsely accused of something, and I'm not going to stand for it," she yelled, spurred on by fear and unable to stop herself. She knew she should just walk away and sort it out later, maybe when Martha was in on Monday. She wanted to quit, to throw the badge and the identification in Ron's face, but then they'd all think she was guilty. She wasn't about to give anyone that pleasure.

"Don't—" Ron started to say.

"No, you don't!" she shouted, interrupting him. "Don't you ever lay your hand on me or another female employee ever again. If you do, I'll yell sexual harassment and see how long it takes them to kick your butt out of here."

She saw fear in the man's eyes, and like a shark smelling blood in the water, she went in for the kill. "Yeah, how does that sound, huh? Doesn't feel so good being the one on the receiving end of the accusation, does it? If you know what's good for you, you'll stay as far away from me as you can. I want to speak to Martha. She's my supervisor, not you. She'll help me straighten this mess out because I DON'T DO DRUGS!"

Vaguely she heard someone shouting her name. "Candace! Slow down, it's okay!"

She turned, and her eyes fastened on Josh. Suddenly she could feel tears stinging the back of her eyes, but she refused to cry in front of a room full of people—and especially in front of Ron.

"Did you hear what this idiot accused me of?" she asked Josh.

He nodded. "We all heard, and we all know that there is no way you do drugs. So, let's just get out of here, and I'll make sure this whole mess gets straightened out." She looked into his eyes, and she trusted him. He would make it okay. She believed him. He was Josh, and he had never steered her wrong. He was a good friend. She nodded slowly.

He put his arm around her shoulders, and together they walked out. Candace refused to look at anyone for fear she'd lose it, but she just stared straight ahead, jaw set and body quivering with anger.

Josh walked her all the way out to her car, and she was grateful for his support. Once there, she turned to him. "I didn't take any drugs."

"I know," he assured her.

"Thank you."

"Just go home and try to relax. I'm sure this will all be straightened out by Monday. Think of it this way: you actually get a weekend off."

"Yeah," she managed to say weakly. Another fear rose up in her mind.

"What will Kurt think?"

"Kurt will know this is just as bogus as I do."

She nodded and wiped the tears from her eyes.

"See you in a couple days?"

"Yes," she said, getting in her car.

She started the engine and drove off, noticing that Josh watched her out of sight. He was a great guy. As she headed home, she tried to think what she would tell her parents. How could she break it to them without them going postal on her?

When she walked in the door, she could tell they were way beyond postal. They were both sitting, facing the front door, legs crossed. In her mother's hand was a letter, and she could just guess at what it said.

"It's not true," she blurted out. "I just got to work and they told me, and I told them that it was impossible. I've never done drugs. Josh told me that they would figure everything out Monday when my supervisor gets back. There's this girl at work who hates me and tried to get me in trouble a few days ago. I think she might have something to do with it. And then a guy named Ron grabbed me, and I told him if he touched me again I would sue him for sexual harassment." The words came flowing out of her right before she burst into tears and sat down on the floor.

Her parents were silent but Candace was beyond caring. This just had to be the worst day of her life, and it wasn't over yet. All she wanted to do was climb into bed with Mr. Huggles, pull the covers over her head, and pray for the nightmare to end. Maybe she would wake up, and it would still be May, and she would have never gotten a job at The Zone. She would let Tamara pay for everything all summer, no matter how mad her dad got, because anything had to be better than this.

It seemed a long, long time before she heard her dad, his voice floating somewhere above her. "Did this Ron hurt you?"

She lifted her head and looked at him through her tears. He was next to her, down on one knee, and he had his scary lawyer face on. She shook her head slowly. "He just scared me when he grabbed me, but he didn't hurt me. I wanted to throw my badge in his face and tell him I quit, but I was afraid that if I did, then everyone would think I really did do the drugs and nobody would straighten it all out."

She felt a hand brush her cheek, and she turned to see her mom kneeling on the other side of her. "I think you better tell us everything, starting from the beginning," her mom said.

It took two hours, but Candace managed to tell them everything that had happened from the day she had started work at The Zone. Her dad had been furious when he heard about how she had been injured on the railroad tracks, and her mother had some harsh words about Lisa. At some point they all moved into the kitchen where they continued talking over bowls of ice cream.

Just about the time she was finished with her narrative, the doorbell rang. Her mother rose to get it, and her father gripped her hand tightly. Her mother came back a moment later.

"It seems you have a visitor," she said.

Candace looked up as Josh followed her mom into the kitchen. She stared at him, slack jawed. If he had produced a hat and pulled a rabbit out of it, she couldn't have been more surprised. "Hey, Candace. I got your address from Kurt. I hope you don't mind."

She shook her head.

"Mr. and Mrs. Thompson, I apologize for my appearance—I came straight from work."

Both her parents nodded as if his surfer attire and the very fact of his presence were completely normal to them.

"My name is Josh, and I work at The Zone with Candace. I just wanted you to know that none of us who know her believe that she has had any involvement with drugs whatsoever. In fact, it looks like there might have been something wrong with all the tests they did that day because several others'—even the park president's—tests indicated drug use. They've got people working right now trying to figure out what went wrong. I just wanted to let all of you know as soon as I could."

"We appreciate that, Josh," Candace's father said, looking approvingly at him.

"I also heard that the supervisor who grabbed Candace today is in a lot of trouble. He might not have a job anymore."

"I should hope so," her dad said.

"Well, if I hear anything else tomorrow, I'll be sure to let you know." He turned to leave but Candace's mother spoke up.

"Thank you, Josh. Would you like to stay for dinner?"

"If it wouldn't be an imposition and if Candace wouldn't mind," he said, eyeing her.

Candace finally found her voice. "Please do," she said.

Both her parents nodded, and he grinned. "Thank you, I believe I will."

It had ended up being one of the strangest days of her entire life. She had gone from sobbing hysterically on the floor of the entryway to laughing hysterically with Josh and her parents around the kitchen table. He had stayed until late, and they had played some board games. It was one of the best nights of her life. It was strange how things could change so dramatically in just a few hours.

It turned out her parents had believed her right away, but they did lecture her later about not telling them when bad things happened, especially at work. They even hinted that it would be okay if she quit her job. Her dad was still mad that the park didn't fire Pete after he tried to run people down. Candace was tempted to quit her job since she had her parents' blessing, but decided to give it a couple of days.

She tried calling Tamara before she went to bed, but she got her voicemail. She left a short message.

God, help me know what to do about work, she prayed. After a moment she added, *And Tamara too. I don't know what's going on with her.*

She kissed Mr. Huggles on his nose and fell asleep.

12

In the morning she checked her phone, but there were no messages. While she wasn't really in the mood to talk to anybody else, she did want to talk to Tamara. She tried calling Tam's phone but hung up when she got the recording. She chewed on her lip for a moment before finally calling the house.

The maid answered.

"Hi, Rosa. This is Candace. I was wondering if Tamara's there?"

"No, Miss Tamara is out. I believe she was going to get coffee."

"Thanks, Rosa," Candace said before hanging up. If Tamara was going out for coffee, there was only one place she would be. Candace quickly got dressed and hurried over to the Coffee Garden, their favorite coffee hangout. Surrounded on three corners by Starbucks stores, the Coffee Garden managed to survive by offering great coffee and incredibly fast service. They also had the comfiest chairs and couches around.

Candace was relieved when she saw Tamara's car in the parking lot, because it meant she was still there. She parked and then rushed inside, anxious to tell Tamara everything that had happened. It took her a while to see Tamara because the shop was crowded and she had expected to see her alone, not sitting with a guy, and especially not sitting with Kurt.

Candace stared, stunned. There, in the far corner, were Kurt and Tamara sitting on a couch, their heads close together. She could tell Tamara was laughing at something he was saying, and she had her hand on his.

Candace felt like she had been punched in the stomach and was going to be sick. She had wondered why Kurt hadn't tried to call to find out if she was okay. Now she understood. Why would he waste time on her if he could spend it with Tamara? She thought about going over and confronting them but felt too overwhelmed. She could hear people laughing around her, and a couple at a nearby table glanced her way. It was as though everybody in the place was staring at her, like they knew that she'd been dumped and they were laughing. She turned and ran back outside.

Inside the car, she pounded the steering wheel with her fist. "God, I know life isn't fair, but what's the deal?" she cried. "Tell me what I'm supposed to do."

She sat for a long time. The clock said 8:30, and she stared at it for a minute. It took her a moment to remember that it was Sunday. Since she couldn't go to work today, it meant she could go to church. She wasn't exactly dressed for it, but she drove there anyway.

Once inside she breathed a heavy sigh, trying to connect with the peace of the place. "Candace, aren't you working?" a girl from her youth group asked as she walked by.

"Not today," Candace answered, trying not to grimace. The last thing she wanted to do was talk to anybody about The Zone or Kurt or anything. She just wanted to feel some semblance of normality, to believe that everything was going to be okay.

She chose a seat in the back, far from where she normally sat, and let the music wash over her. She saw her parents enter the sanctuary, but she didn't want to talk to them either, so she slunk down farther in her seat. The sermon, it turned out, was on loving your neighbor as yourself. It did little to improve Candace's mood.

Fortunately, a special musical group was giving a mini-concert. This meant that the sermon was short and that the rest of the service was taken up by music. Candace half listened. The group was good, and their drummer was fantastic. The songs were mostly nothing special, until they started singing a ballad.

Candace closed her eyes. The music was soothing, and the words talked about letting God's love wash away the pain. Her tears began to flow freely as she listened.

Why, God? My best friend and my boyfriend? My only real friend and my first boyfriend! This is a nightmare. If this is what becoming a mature, responsible adult is about, I want no part of it! Being an adult means having to do a bunch of things you don't want to with people who are mean and accuse you of terrible things.

She hurt so badly she thought she might die sitting right there in the pew. Suddenly someone tapped her on the shoulder. She opened her eyes and saw a little girl, probably about nine, who was staring at her very solemnly.

"These are for you," the little girl said, thrusting a handful of tissues at Candace.

"Thank you," Candace said, taking a tissue and beginning to wipe her eyes.

"I saw you from over there," the little girl said, pointing to the pew across the aisle.

Candace had seen the little girl nearly every Sunday for years, but she didn't know her name. "How did you know to bring me these?" she asked. It was a lame question, but she was embarrassed by the fact that she didn't know the girl's name.

"I could tell you were crying. It's okay, you know. God understands when you cry in his house. Nobody can be happy all the time. Last year when my mom died I cried every Sunday for a month."

The little girl gave her a brave smile and then scurried back over to sit next to her father. Candace stared after her in shock. *It's true. No matter how bad things look, there is always someone worse off,* she thought. *Thanks for the perspective, God.*

She continued to dry her tears, and at the end of the service she slipped out quietly with a wave to the little girl. She spent the rest of the day trying not to think about Kurt and Tamara.

Sometime around four, the phone rang and a minute later her mother came upstairs and handed her the house phone. "It's for you," she said.

"Who is it?"

"I didn't ask."

"Hello, this is Candace."

"Candace, this is Martha from The Zone."

"Hi, Martha," Candace said, her stomach twisting in knots. She hadn't expected Martha to be at work until Monday. They must have called her at home.

"Are you okay?"

Candace took a deep breath. "I'm better than I was yesterday," she admitted.

"That probably wouldn't take much," Martha said.

"Yeah. I kind of lost it."

"With good reason, so I hear."

"So, what's the news?" Candace asked, dreading the answer.

"First, a question. Have you ever tried the muffins at the Muffin Mansion?"

It seemed like a strange question. "Sure, they're great. I love the chocolate with the chocolate chips. They've got this new lemony one that's really good too."

"That's what I thought," Martha said.

"Why?"

"Well, a couple of the employees of the Muffin Mansion also tested positive. It seems that everyone who tested positive, including you, has been eating their brand-new lemon poppy-seed muffins. It turns out, poppy seeds can make you test positive for drug use, since they come from the same plant that opium does."

"Seriously?"

"Yes."

"I told that guy I didn't do drugs," Candace said, relief flooding her to know the cause of the test results.

"I know, and several of your coworkers argued quite persuasively in your defense before the wider problem was discovered."

"So, I can come back to work then."

"Yes."

"So Tuesday then?"

"Actually tomorrow. New schedules came out Saturday. You just didn't have a chance to see yours."

"Oh, what are my hours?"

"Monday through Thursday eight to five, Saturday ten to seven."

Candace blinked, not sure she had heard right. "Those are great hours," she said at last.

"Yeah, you got really lucky," Martha said.

"So, that's it? Everything's good?"

"Yes."

"What about Ron?" Candace asked.

"Let's just say you won't have any interactions with him again. You're under my supervision, and if you need to know something, I'll be the one to tell you."

"Thank you," Candace said.

As soon as she hung up, she ran downstairs to tell her parents the good news. They were overjoyed, but not nearly half as much as she was. She was also excited about her new schedule. Fridays and Sundays off so rocked! She ran back upstairs and picked up her cell to call Tamara, then stopped, remembering what had happened that morning. She felt a stab of pain, but pushed it aside, refusing to let it spoil her victory. She remembered the brave little girl in church and dialed the phone. It would be better to get the confrontation with Tamara over with so that they could hopefully move on with their lives.

It went straight to voice mail, so she hung up and called Josh.

"I told you everything would be okay," he said as soon as he heard her news.

"You were right, thank you. And thanks for coming over last night. That was awesome. My parents went on about how thoughtful you are."

He laughed. "Parents always like me."

"How do you manage that?"

"I'm honest, respectful, and not afraid of them."

"It's Josh magic," she teased.

"Call it what you like, it works. So, are you going out to celebrate?"

"I don't know. I guess I should."

"Absolutely."

"What would you recommend?" she asked.

"A quick trip to Zone World in Florida with dinner at On Top of the World."

"Very funny. It would be breakfast by the time we got there."

"Okay, then, breakfast with the dolphins at Marine Zone."

"Sorry, work in the morning."

"Well, then, I'd have to say pizza and a movie."

"Sounds great! Which pizza place should I meet you at?"

There was a pause and then he asked, "Are you sure I'm the one you want to celebrate with?"

"Absolutely. You're the one that was there for me when things looked bad. You should be able to share the good times too."

"Works for me. How about California Pizza Kitchen in thirty?"

"See you there," she said.

It was nearly ten when Candace made it home, stuffed to the gills with gourmet pizza and carrying a to-go box with several slices in it. She had bet Josh she could eat more pizza than him and had lost by several slices. Loser brought home the left-overs, though, so it felt a lot more like winning than losing. It had felt really good just to be out and to be silly. As soon as she made it home, though, reality came crashing back in.

Her phone rang and she flipped it open without looking at the caller ID.

"Hey," she said.

"Hi," Tamara replied.

"Oh, hi, Tamara," Candace said, her good mood evaporating.

"What's up?" Tamara asked.

"I might ask you the same question, but I already know the answer," Candace said, barely controlling her anger.

"What are you talking about?"

"Don't act coy. I saw you this morning at the Coffee Garden with Kurt."

"Yeah, what of it?" Tamara asked, her voice cold.

"I didn't think you'd resort to stealing my boyfriend."

"Stealing? Girl, you are crazy. We ran into each other and we were talking about you. Which you would have known had you bothered to come over."

Candace was silent for a moment, pondering what she had just heard. Could it be true? If it wasn't, why would Tamara lie when she had caught them together? Then again, why had it taken more than a day for Tamara to return any of her phone calls?

She voiced the last question. "Then why have you been avoiding me and not returning my calls?"

"I don't owe you an explanation for anything. Besides, I'm re-turning your call now, aren't I? And you know, how dare you think I would steal your guy? I'm not that kind of person, and I would have thought you of all people would know better than that."

"Well, you've been doing a lot of things lately that I don't get," Candace said. "You've been blowing me off all summer."

"I've been blowing *you* off? Please, you're the one who's so wrapped up in her new job and new friends that you don't have any time for me."

"That is not even true! And what, you want me to be miserable all day at my job and hate everyone there?"

"Yes!"

"Well maybe if you'd answer your phone once in a while you'd get to hear how crappy my life has been. Where were you when I needed you? 'Cause you certainly weren't anywhere to be found."

"Tell it to one of your new friends."

"I guess I'll have to because it seems I lost my old one."

"Seems so."

"Fine," Candace said, on the verge of tears.

"Fine," Tamara said.

There was a click as Tamara hung up. Candace grabbed Mr. Huggles and began to cry.

13

The sun was already broiling at eight thirty in the morning, and Candace was sweating. Her pink and white-striped blouse was sticking to her uncomfortably, and she was afraid that it was starting to become semi-transparent. It was going to be one of those days, she just knew it. Josh walked by, and she envied him his shorts and tank top. "I should have signed up in March," she muttered under her breath.

It was the Fourth of July, and for the first time her cart was in the Holiday Zone. She credited the new sights and sounds with being the only things keeping her sane in the heat. In the Holiday Zone every amusement got a holiday-themed overhaul every couple of months. The massive hedge maze was the center of The Zone, and was currently festooned with red, white, and blue bunting and patriotic quotes and slogans.

A live stage show featuring the park's cartoon mascots Freddie McFly and the Swamp Swingers, along with Freddie's friend Mr. Nine Lives the daredevil cat, began every hour and a half in the largest building in the Holiday Zone. The line to get in and see the air-conditioned show had already wrapped around the building. For the Fourth of July, Freddie and his gang were doing a tribute to the Founding Fathers of America.

Candace couldn't help but wonder about the founding mothers of America and whether they spent their evenings angry at their husbands for coming home late and missing dinner. She had visions of Deborah Franklin clubbing Ben over the head with her rolling pin and complaining to her friends that he was always out late plotting revolution with his buddies instead of home taking out the trash.

As the sun climbed higher in the sky, Candace became more and more uncomfortable. There was a giant shade tree fifteen feet away, but Candace couldn't figure out how to force the cart to roll over into its shade. She tried pushing and then pulling it, but the large cart was too heavy to move. That was probably one of the reasons why it was motorized.

To make matters worse, no one came to relieve her until her lunch break. By then she was panting from the heat and fanning herself with empty cones. Her replacement turned out to be Lisa, who glared daggers at her. Candace wondered why Lisa was hopping around giving people breaks. Could this be some sort of punishment from Martha? Candace shrugged, too miserable to think about it any longer. She made her way as fast as she could offstage and headed for the cantina.

It was the first time Candace had ever actually eaten inside the cantina. She made her way to the counter, got a plate of fried chicken and potato salad, and grabbed a jumbo bottled water. The air conditioning was a blessing after the extreme heat outside. She paid for her food and then eyed the sea of tables with people sitting around them looking for an empty space. It looked like she wasn't the only one who had opted to eat indoors in the air conditioning.

A hand went up in the air, and a moment later she recognized Sue waving her over. Candace picked her way over and gratefully sank down into the chair opposite Sue. "Thanks."

"Not a problem. You look like you've been having quite the day."

Candace shook her head. "It's the heat. It's brutal out there."

Sue shook her head. "It's the first day all summer I've been grateful to be cleaning restrooms. At least it's cool."

"Wanna trade?" Candace asked hopefully.

"Nope, it's supposed to get hotter every day this week."

"Great."

"You've got sunscreen, right?"

"No, why?" Candace asked.

"Your arms are burnt."

Candace looked down and discovered the telltale signs of red skin on both her arms. "Oh no."

"They sell sunscreen in most of the shops. You should grab some before you go back out there."

"Thanks. This is so not good," Candace said.

"At least you caught it before it got too bad. I saw a woman in the restroom earlier who is on the fast track to a second-degree burn."

"Eew. I guess I am lucky."

"Definitely."

Candace began to eat slowly. The food was good, but she was too hot to be very interested in anything but her water. Sue had returned her attention to a pile of papers she was shuffling through.

"What is that?" Candace asked finally.

"Class registration. I'm starting at Cal State in a few weeks."

"Cool. I'm thinking of going there," Candace said. "I'm a senior this year, and I have to start applying in a couple of months."

"It seems like a good school. I'm keeping my fingers crossed."

"Why did you pick it?"

"I needed something close to home." For just a moment the saddest expression crossed her face. Candace was about to ask her about it when Sue stood up. "Well, that was lunch," she said, her voice cheery. "At least I can swap an air-conditioned restaurant for an air-conditioned restroom."

"We should all be so lucky," Candace groaned.

"Make sure you get some sunscreen on," Sue said, gathering her papers and heading for the door.

"Sunscreen. Check."

A few minutes later it was time for Candace to go, especially if she planned on picking up the sunscreen. She retrieved some money from her locker and stopped at the first sundry cart she passed. She bought a bottle of SPF 50 and smeared it on her arms, face, and neck. She took the bottle to her locker, used the restroom, and made it back to her cart five minutes late. Lisa gave her a dirty look.

"I didn't get a morning break, so I'm entitled to five extra minutes," Candace said.

She got another dirty look before Lisa trudged off. "And if she has anything to say about it, I won't be getting an afternoon break, either," Candace confided to her cart.

The temperature was by now over one hundred, and Candace noticed that the drink and ice-cream carts were getting a lot more customers than her cart or the popcorn and churro ones. "Can't say I blame them. In this heat I don't want to *smell* cotton candy, let alone have it sticking all over my hands."

She hoped the cart would move soon, preferably somewhere where there was some shade. Maybe if she ended up in the Splash Zone she could get Josh to dump a bucket of water over her.

Over in the line for the Founding Fathers of America, two guys began to scuffle. Angry words carried through the warm air. Quick as lightning, security descended and broke it up. Tempers were short and someone in the crowd yelled at one of the security guards.

"Make love, not war, I always say," a slippery-sounding male voice spoke close to her ear.

Candace jumped and turned to see a guy in his thirties, covered with piercings, leering at her. "Can I help you?" she asked him.

"Oh, yeah, Candy baby, I'm sure you could." He ran his tongue over his lips and leaned closer.

Her internal creep alarm went off, and she slammed her hand against her red panic button. Moments later the same security officers who had broken up the line fight were at her side, escorting the jerk away. She shuddered as he looked back over his shoulder and made kissing motions at her.

An hour later she heard over her intercom that they had shut the front gates because the park had reached capacity. More than a hundred thousand people were in the park, and the shuffle of bodies only added to the heat and the rising tensions. By the time her afternoon break came around, Candace had witnessed two more fights and numerous family "incidents." The afternoon parade started up, led by a full marching band. It began in the Holiday Zone and wound its way around to end close to the front gates. The music was nearly deafening. Parents were screaming, kids were crying, and Candace's head was pounding.

A guy walked up, and she eyed him suspiciously. The noise of the band was still deafening, so he held up his index finger to indicate one cotton candy. He handed her a bill and she gave him his change before beginning to twirl a cone around the tub.

Finally the band passed and the noise lessened. She handed him the cotton candy as he looked at her name tag.

"Candy. That's a pretty name. Appropriate too, given where you're working. You like it here, Candy?"

"Okay, that's it. I know your type, creep, so just back off. The name is Candace, but even if it was Candy that doesn't give you the right to make insinuations or hit on me or whatever. I've had it. Get out of here before I call security!"

The guy backed off, hands raised in front of him. Nearby, several people had stopped to stare, and with a sinking feeling she saw that one of them was Lisa, who was smirking. Candace turned and walked straight to the nearest break area, ducked into the restroom, and splashed water on her face.

"Not good. So not good," she muttered to herself. She replayed it all in her head and realized that she wasn't completely sure whether he had been insinuating something or had just been friendly. "We're never supposed to yell at players. Never ever. Well, at least now they have an actual reason to fire me."

Ten minutes later Martha found her there. She shouldn't have been surprised. Lisa probably radioed the whole thing in and told Martha where to find her.

"Tough day?"

Candace just laughed bitterly. "Do I seem to have any other kind?"

"No, you've got just about the worst luck of anyone I've ever seen. Well, barring Roger, of course."

"I screwed up," Candace admitted. "I feel like an idiot. You know, I've never gotten into a fight in my life? And now in the last two weeks I've ended up screaming at three different people. What's wrong with me? Do I have some sort of repressed anger issues?"

Martha patted her shoulder. "There's nothing wrong with you. You're just being tried, tested, and pushed to your limits. That can be very painful and often frightening as well. I'd be worried if you didn't blow up every once in a while. At least, to the best of my knowledge, you lose it in appropriate directions."

"That guy?"

"Security's been looking for him for the last two hours since he propositioned an ice-cream referee who's even younger than you."

"Wow, extra creepy."

"Yeah."

"But?" Candace asked.

Martha shrugged. "You still yelled at a player. Several other players have already complained."

"Great. So am I totally fired?"

Martha laughed. "No. Usually you'd be suspended for four days. However, since you've had your share of false accusations lately, I'm going to let you off with a one-day suspension."

"Tomorrow?"

"No, whatever you have left of today."

"But that's only two hours."

Martha smirked. "Then I'd say you got off lucky. Now get out of here. The hottest part of the day is still ahead of us, and I'm sure you'd like to miss that."

Candace hugged Martha before taking off. She managed to make it home in twenty minutes, which had to be some kind of record. She stripped out of her sweaty uniform and donned cool shorts and a tank top. She put aloe on her burned arms and settled down with a book to enjoy her air-conditioned room.

A couple hours later her parents headed out to their friends' house for their annual Fourth of July barbeque. Candace was not in the mood to celebrate. She missed Tamara and still couldn't understand what had happened between them. They usually spent the Fourth of July together laughing and stuffing their faces with hot dogs. It just didn't seem right without her.

"You're sure you don't want to come?" her mother asked as she was leaving.

"I'll be fine. Besides, I might go out later with some friends," Candace said, mostly to reassure her mom.

"Okay, have a good evening, honey," her dad said.

She had the house to herself, and she celebrated by eating cake for dinner. She had just settled onto the couch with the remote control when there was a knock at the door.

She ran to see who it was and surprised to see Kurt standing on the doorstep. She opened the door. "Come in," she invited him.

He came inside, looking around as though worried about where her parents were. "They're out," she said after a few seconds.

"Oh," he said, visibly relaxing.

"What's up?"

"I just came to see if you were okay. I heard what happened today."

"About how the creepy guy hit on me and I yelled at him, or that I got suspended?"

"All of it," he said.

She shrugged. "I'm fine. Much better than when that supervisor accused me of taking drugs."

Kurt nodded. She felt like asking him why he hadn't come by then but decided not to look a gift horse in the mouth. He was here now, and that was what was important.

"So, I was wondering," he asked after a moment. "Would you like to take a walk to the park?"

"The Zone?" she asked.

"No, the park park. You know, grass, trees, swings. There's going to be a fireworks display a little later."

"Sure, that would be great. Just give me a minute." Candace ran upstairs to put on her tennis shoes. She stuffed some cash in her pocket just in case. She could put her key in the other pocket and be purse free. She was headed back downstairs when she realized that this was technically their second date.

She froze halfway down, wondering if she should go back upstairs and change, or at least put on makeup, brush her teeth, or something. But he had already seen her and was waiting by the front door ready to go. Too late. Candace continued down the stairs, grabbed her key off the hook near the door, and they were off.

The park was only four blocks from her house. The sun hadn't set yet, and the air was very warm, but not nearly as scorching as it had been earlier in the day. Candace's burned arms were beginning to tingle, and she was grateful that she had applied sunscreen when she did.

As they walked they chatted. Kurt had a wealth of knowledge about esoteric history trivia, thanks to his time spent working in that part of The Zone. She thought she could listen to him tell stories and anecdotes for hours and never get bored.

When he paused, she asked, "So, did Deborah ever beat Benjamin Franklin with a rolling pin?"

"What?" he asked. "Where did you hear that?"

"Nowhere," she laughed. "It was something I made up earlier today."

"Okay, clearly you are seriously deranged," he said, also laughing.

Laughing felt nice. Actually anything that wasn't crying or screaming felt nice. When they reached the park, they hunted until they found a nice grassy spot with a clear view of the sky.

"I should have brought something for us to sit on," Kurt said.

"A little dirt and grass never hurt," she said, finding a place on the cool ground.

The sun began to set and the moon shimmered on the horizon. "I'd love to travel to the moon someday," she said. "Do you think we'll ever have a chance to?"

"I don't know, maybe. Did you know that Robert E. Lee's horse was named Traveller?"

"Really?" she asked.

"Yeah. Someone even wrote a historical novel from his point of view."

"From the horse's. Seriously?"

"Yup. Richard Adams, same guy that wrote *Watership Down*, wrote the book."

"Wow. That is cool and bizarre. Have you read it?"

"No. It's on my list, though."

"What else is on your list?"

"Lots of stuff. Look, it's dark."

He was right. The sun had finally set, and the skies were dark. He glanced at his watch. "Fireworks should start any minute now."

As if on command, a rocket burst in the night sky, signaling the start of the show. Candace watched for a moment in rapt amazement. Pink, purple, green, red, blue, and white bursts lit the sky, some exploding with a bang and others with a sizzle. Candace thought briefly of Tamara. They had been watching fireworks together since they were four. She wondered what Tamara was doing tonight. She forced her thoughts away from her old friend and onto the light show above her.

Candace had always been amazed by the beauty of fireworks, and she marveled more the older she got. Sometimes a single rocket went up by itself while others exploded in groups of three and four. She admired the people who spent so much time orchestrating something so unique, so beautiful. It made her ache inside.

"Beautiful, isn't it?" she asked.

"Very much so," Kurt answered.

She turned and saw that he was staring at her instead of the fireworks. Her breath caught as she stared at him, so close in the darkness. He bent close and kissed her just like in a fairy tale, and the fireworks continued to shine and sparkle and boom around them as time itself stood still.

14

The next day was supposed to be even hotter than the Fourth, but they lucked out and continuous cloud cover all day kept the air much cooler. Candace was still prepared, though, and was wearing plenty of sunscreen. Her arms were only mildly pink from the day before, and she wanted to keep it that way.

About halfway through her day, Martha came by to check on her. "Now remember, if some guy harasses you—"

"I push the red button," Candace said.

"And if someone starts something—"

"I push the red button."

"And if someone pushes your buttons?"

"Then I definitely push the red button."

"Very good," Martha said. "Now that you've passed that little test, would you be up for something different?"

"Like what?"

"A week from Thursday there's a big private event being held at the picnic grounds. I'd like you to help with the food service."

"You mean with the cart?"

"No, with the barbeque—ferrying meat back and forth, along with buns, condiments, etc. It would be the same hours, and it would be something different."

"Sure, I could do that," she said.

"Great. Next Thursday, report over at the picnic grounds at eight a.m. They'll tell you what to do."

"Okay."

"Well, then, think you can handle things here?" Martha asked.

"So far so good," Candace said.

"And if you get in trouble ..."

"Push the red button," they said together.

"I promise, no more yelling, just button pushing," Candace said.

"Good girl. Call if you need me."

"I will," Candace assured her.

When her lunch break came, Candace hurried over to a bench outside the cantina where she and Kurt had agreed to meet for lunch. He grabbed them a couple of sandwiches and sodas and settled down next to her to eat.

"This is nice," she said. "It's like a date in the middle of the workday."

He laughed. "You think this is nice, just you wait."

"Oh yeah, for what?"

"I want to take you out tomorrow night," Kurt said.

"Awesome. When?"

"Right after work. Is that cool?"

"Sure, I'll just need to run home and change clothes."

He shook his head. "Bring clothes to change into and then meet me in the Locker Room."

"Okay. Where are we going?" she asked, hoping to at least have an idea how she should dress this time.

He smiled and shook his head. "It's a surprise."

She wondered briefly if they had reached a stage in their relationship where she could ask him if she should go casual or dressy. She wasn't sure, but she decided to risk it. "Should I be thinking jeans and a T-shirt or something nice?" she asked.

"Something like what you wore on our first date would be great," he said. "By the way, did I tell you how great you looked?"

"I'm not sure," she teased. "Better tell me again."

He leaned closer. "You ..." and he kissed her, "looked ..." another kiss, "great." He ended with a really big kiss.

She pursed her lips as if thinking about something. Finally she said, "You know, I couldn't quite hear you."

He laughed and kissed her one last time. "How's your hearing now?"

"It seems to be improving. Maybe if you spoke just a little bit louder."

He wrapped his arms around her and then dipped her backwards and gave her a huge kiss and then sat her back up. "Are you good now, or should I think about getting you a hearing aid?"

"No, I think I'm good," she said, moistening her lips.

He laughed and she joined him. It was good to have a boyfriend. It was great to have one that was such a good kisser. Lunch was over long before she was ready, and with a sigh she returned to the cart where she sold a lot more cotton candy than the day before when it had been so hot.

Later that night she enlisted her mom's help again in picking out what to wear. After much discussion they picked out a royal blue skirt and a white blouse with sheer, billowy sleeves. A pair of white slingbacks completed the look, and Candace finally crawled into bed satisfied that she would sufficiently impress Kurt.

The next day found her in the Splash Zone again. She hadn't had the chance to talk to Josh in a couple of days, and she was eager to catch up. Now that she and Tamara weren't speaking, he was her closest friend.

"Our team is going to be pretty hard to beat at the Scavenger Hunt this year," he bragged.

"Oh yeah, and why's that?"

"We've been working out," he said.

"You've got to be kidding."

"Nope, we're each jogging five miles or more a day."

"Does a silly scavenger hunt really mean that much to you?" she asked.

And she knew instantly just how wrong she had been to ask that. He looked at her, and his eyes showed a mixture of surprise and hurt.

"It's not just a silly scavenger hunt. It's the heart of what The Zone is all about. This entire park was founded on the ideals of hard work, team effort, striving for excellence, and the spirit of physical and mental improvement through play and competition. What you see as mere games and sports, I see as avenues to challenge and improve myself as an individual and a member of society, the largest, hardest-hitting team of all.

"The Scavenger Hunt embodies all of that. It's a test of memory, skill, quick thinking, and observation that requires you to work successfully with other people in the tightest quarters under very stressful conditions. It's not a game; it's a test of character and a great team-building experience. It's the glue that binds us all together and proves that it is something special to work and play here. So, yes, it means that much to me. And, no, it's not silly."

"I'm sorry, I wasn't thinking," Candace said.

He was staring at her intently, eyes burning with passion. After a moment he smiled, and it was as though he shook off the zeal and was once again carefree surfer Josh. "It's cool," he said.

"I liked what you said. It kinda made sense to me. I've always just seen this as another theme park, and I never really thought of it as a testing ground."

He smiled. "Most don't, but that's the beauty of it. Did you know that more history and science is taught here everyday than in most classrooms in this country? Do you know how many of the scientists who do demonstrations over in the Exploration

Zone first got inspired by science when they visited here as high school students? Most of them."

"Wow. You're like half referee, half player."

He smiled. "We're called Zoners. That's the name for those of us who work *and* play here."

She smiled. "It suits you."

He shrugged and gave her his lopsided smile. "Now, let me tell you why your team is going to get pummeled in the Scavenger Hunt."

She laughed. "Oh ho, starting with the smack talk are you?"

"Not at all. Just speaking facts."

"And what facts would those be?"

"Two of you are new to the place."

"Beginner's luck we'll have in spades," she countered.

"One of you tries to kill others."

"But not the people on his train. And since we'll be tied together, we'll be like his train, which means he'll only try to kill the rest of you," she said smugly.

"Nice."

"Thank you."

"Did you just come up with that?"

"Yeah, pretty much."

"Impressive."

"Thank you."

"You are forgetting two other important factors."

"Which are?"

"One of you is a saboteur."

"Ah, yes, but Lisa is also self-serving. She would rather win at all costs. Therefore, we will be the only team safe from her machinations."

"Possibly, possibly. However, even if all you've said is true, there's no escaping—"

"Destiny?"

"Roger," he said with grim satisfaction.

"Is he really as klutzy as people say?" Candace asked.

"Worse. I once saw him knock down a whole line of people just like dominoes."

"Oh."

"Uh huh."

"But he can't be bad all the time."

"Dominoes."

"Well, we can give it our best at any rate," Candace said.

"Go down fighting. That's the referee way."

She took a deep breath. Sure, on paper they might have the worst team imaginable, but that didn't mean they couldn't overcome it. After all, look at how many obstacles she'd overcome already.

"In the spirit of competition, I'll make a bet with you, Josh."

"Really?" he said, raising an eyebrow. "This wouldn't be like the who-can-eat-more-pizza thing, would it? Because I could have told you you were going to lose that one."

"No, this is not like the pizza. I'll bet you that our team beats your team."

He snorted. "You haven't got a chance."

"Chicken?" she asked.

"You've got a deal."

"And the loser buys the winner's team pizza."

He laughed. "See, I knew pizza was going to figure in there somehow."

"Yes, but you didn't know how," she said, lifting one eyebrow.

"Cotton Candy, I think you're a little bit crazy."

"Count on it," she said with a smirk.

The rest of the day sped by, and soon Candace waved good-bye to Josh and headed for the Locker Room to grab her clothes. Fifteen minutes later she returned to the Locker Room in her date outfit to find Kurt already waiting. He was wearing black slacks and a white dress shirt with a black tie. Candace was a little surprised. Clearly they were going somewhere special.

"Ready?" he asked, offering her his arm.

"Absolutely," she said.

A moment later she was again surprised when they turned away from the exit to the referee parking lot and walked on field. It felt really weird to be walking through the park dressed like a player.

"Where are we going?" she asked.

"Did you know that unlike most theme parks, The Zone is renowned for the high quality of its food and its number of fine-dining options?"

"I did, actually," Candace said.

It was true. The Zone had great food. There were, of course, carts and counter-service restaurants where you could get all the junk food you could want, such as the cotton candy she served daily. For the more discriminating, though, there was a wealth of fine-dining choices. In fact, the restaurants in The Zone were so popular that the park had a special "connoisseur season ticket," which gave the holder entrance into the park after 5:30 p.m. every day of the year. A lot of commuters left work and headed for the park for dinner before going home. Candace's parents were connoisseur season ticket holders, and they often went to one of the restaurants in The Zone.

So, Kurt had one of the restaurants in mind. The question was, which one? Candace tried to guess. It quickly became clear that they were heading for the History Zone. She instantly ruled out the Chuck Wagon, King Tut's, King Richard's Feast, and Poor Richard's Pub because none of them was fancy enough to cause Kurt to wear a tie. Boone's, the restaurant on the top floor of the Fort, was also not a likely destination because it was black tie and required you to be on some special list, or know someone who was, in order to get in. While it was not impossible that Kurt could have found a way to get them a reservation, neither of them was dressed well enough to eat there.

That left only one real choice, and as they crossed the bridge into Ancient Greece, Candace knew she was right.

Ancient Greece was located in the lake, separated from Egypt by a narrow channel where the boats for both areas would pass each other. The Greece boat ride was called The Odyssey and was definitely a more thrilling adventure than most boat rides.

The island itself had an amphitheater at its heart, where plays and other types of entertainment, including re-enactments, debates, and even the occasional sporting event, took place. Scattered around the amphitheater were three other buildings. The largest was the Temple of Hermes, named after the Greek god of merchants, and was the second largest, most extensive shop in the park. Slightly smaller was the building that housed the Labors of Hercules, a magic-motion ride where viewers sat in chairs that moved all around while watching the action on a large screen. The smallest building was Aphrodite's.

Aphrodite's was one of the top restaurants in the park. It was so good that people came from a hundred miles around just to eat there. The Mediterranean fare was light and refreshing, and the ambience was very romantic. The outside of the building looked like a white marble temple, and the tasteful sign held by two cherubs proclaimed that At Aphrodite's It's Valentine's Day Every Day. The white marble motif was continued inside where the walls were decorated with friezes depicting the romantic escapades of the Greek gods. Tiny winged cupids were found throughout. Nightly entertainment consisted of live music and living tableaus.

Candace had eaten there once when she was little, but this was so much cooler than eating there with her parents. She and Kurt were escorted to a semiprivate alcove with curtains draping it.

"This is amazing," Candace said as she took her seat.

"I'm glad you approve," Kurt said.

Within minutes, a waiter had appeared with a bottle of sparkling cider and poured them each a glass. When he departed, Kurt raised his in a toast. "To us and to what is hopefully the most romantic night of your life so far."

Candace raised her glass. Kurt didn't realize that that wouldn't be hard to pull off. After all, until this moment he was responsible for the two most romantic nights of her life. Someday she'd tell him that, but not yet. She was enjoying all his effort.

Still, there were little nagging doubts in the back of her mind. On their first date she had discovered he was a high-school dropout. Did he have any other bombshells for her? After all, they barely knew each other.

"Which character is your favorite to play?" she asked.

He smiled. "Robin Hood."

"Why that one?"

"Because I don't have to wear a mask. It's easier to see what's going on around me. I also like walking up to the little girls dressed as princesses and asking them if they know where Maid Marion is. They always get so excited! Some of the really young ones don't know who Zorro or the Lone Ranger are, but they're all fans of Robin Hood."

"Even the big girls?" she teased.

"Especially the big girls," he said, winking at her.

Candace blushed happily. "So, do they ever see Maid Marion walking around?"

"They tried that out last summer very briefly. It's how I met one of my girlfriends, Veronica."

Veronica. Candace blinked. She knew about Lisa, but who was this Veronica? "Was she your first girlfriend?" she asked.

He smiled. "No, I'd had a couple before her."

A couple? That meant at the very least Candace was girl-friend number five. Was he fickle? Did the girls dump him?

"So, which number am I?" he asked.

She stared intently at the table. "You're my first boyfriend," she said, quietly.

"Really?" he asked, sounding pleased.

"Yeah."

"Well, I am extremely flattered," he said.

She wondered if throwing a dinner roll at him would be appropriate. She decided against it in the end.

"So, what do your parents do?" she asked, changing the subject.

"My dad's a construction worker, and my mom's a waitress," he said. "I've got three brothers. How about you?"

"Only child."

"Wow. It's like we're from completely different worlds," he said, grinning.

No, she and Tamara were from two different worlds. The biggest difference between her family and Kurt's was probably in the education arena. Both her parents had graduate degrees. If Kurt was any indication, his parents probably hadn't gone to college.

"I don't think we're all that different," she said.

But she couldn't really be sure about that. She barely knew him. She didn't even know if he was a Christian. But how did you just casually drop a question like that into the conversation? Her mind began to teem with other questions. She pushed them to the side. She didn't want to get all intense on him. She wasn't shopping for a husband; she was just trying to enjoy a simple date with a guy who liked her too.

15

The closer the Scavenger Hunt got, the more nervous Candace became. It was bad enough that Josh's team was spending time getting in shape by jogging, but what was worse was there were teams far more fanatical than his. With her new schedule, she got to The Zone before the gates officially opened in the morning. Not one, not two, but five teams were there early in the morning getting into shape by running. One person on the team would shout a destination, and the entire group would change direction instantly and race off. More frightening, all five teams were practicing with their members roped together. It was like every morning was a trial run for the real thing.

She had been driven by some competitive urge to challenge Josh and his team, but now she began to think her team would be lucky to survive the event, let alone finish. Just watching them all running around as she set up her cart in the morning made her feel drained. At least it gave her something different to worry about.

She was still upset about her fight with Tamara. Her friend's birthday was in a couple of days, and they should have been celebrating together. The year before they had spent the weekend at San Simeon touring Hearst Castle and playing at the beach. She wondered where Tamara's parents were taking her this year and whether or not she had found a new friend to go along with them. It seemed hard to believe that they'd been friends since kindergarten and in just a couple of weeks it was over. Friendships didn't end like that, did they? It was just a fight. Shouldn't they say they were sorry and forgive each other? It's what God would want. There was a verse about not letting the sun go down on your anger, and she thought about it every night while she was falling asleep. A dozen times Candace had thought about calling, but she was still too hurt to do so. Tamara was a Christian too, and she didn't seem to feel the need to call. Hadn't Tamara been the unreasonable one? Shouldn't she have to call first? Candace wanted to make everything all right, but every time she reached for the phone her own pain and anger were too much for her.

At least things were going well with Kurt. It bothered her a little bit that it was easier to talk and confide with Josh than Kurt, but she thought that they were probably more naturally reserved and nervous around each other because they were dating. Well, that, and kissing was a lot more fun than talking. She was also still bothered about his lack of forethought about the future. For all she knew she was just a summer fling to him, and he would forget about her once she was in school and he wasn't. Those kinds of thoughts only led to more discontent, so she thought it best to avoid them whenever possible. Her last summer of high school was already more than half over, and she intended to get as much enjoyment out of the second half as she possibly could. Except for missing Tamara. Josh was awesome, but as cool as he was and as easy to talk to, he could never replace her.

Wednesday afternoon as Candace was about to get off work and head home, Martha swung by her cart.

"Just a reminder, you're working the event tomorrow over in the picnic area."

"Don't you mean the Party Zone?" Candace joked.

Martha smirked. "Very good."

"I can't be the first person to think of that name; I mean, come on."

"You know, I'm not sure," Martha said. "Anyway, tomorrow—"

"I won't forget," Candace assured her. "It's my one shot to do something different."

"Feeling pretty cocky since you mastered the mysteries of the cart, huh?" Martha asked, a twinkle in her eye.

"You might say that. Certainly feeling more adventurous."

"Good enough. Good luck tomorrow."

"Thanks."

Later that night, while IMing with Josh, she noticed that Tamara was online for the first time in days. She thought about sending her a quick happy-early-birthday message but decided against it. Her birthday wasn't until Friday. Maybe she'd send her an ecard. She thought about surfing for a good one, but glanced at the clock and realized that she needed to get some sleep if she didn't want to be dead on her feet in the morning. After saying good night to Josh she signed off.

In the morning Candace reported early to the picnic grounds. Decorators were already there setting up with what looked to be hundreds of helium balloons. Tables were set up to accommodate about fifty guests, and there was a stage for live entertainment. It looked like it was going to be some party.

A man in a chef's apron walked up to her. "You're Candace, right?" he asked, holding out his hand.

"Yes," she said, shaking it.

"Great, I'm Murphy. Grab a serving uniform from that rack over there and meet me back here in twenty."

Candace moved to the rack and discovered that the serving uniforms for the women resembled the serving wench costumes from Medieval Times. She grabbed one that appeared to be her size and held it up to herself.

"Nice, huh?" said Glenda, one of the girls who ran an ice-cream cart, rolling her eyes as she found one for herself.

"All I have to say is that if it's as low cut as I think it is, I'm not wearing it," Candace said. "I don't care. I draw the line at that."

"You and me both. Check this place out, though. Someone spent a bundle on this."

"That's for sure," Candace said. "The Party Zone never looked so good."

"I like that! You should tell that name to someone in management. It makes perfect sense. I don't know why no one's ever thought of it before."

"It seems like a no-brainer to me," Candace said.

They retreated to the nearest restroom and changed their clothes. Together they surveyed the damage.

"Why on earth do we have to wear these?" Candace asked.

"I've worked these things before. The planners have like a dozen uniform choices to choose between. Obviously this group opted for the medieval theme. The ones that look like band uniforms are so much better."

"How did you get your bra straps not to show?" Candace asked, frustrated as she tried to tuck the left one under her sleeve for the third time.

"Safety pins. Never leave home without them. Here, let me fix it for you."

A minute later everything was pinned in place, and Candace turned back to the mirror. The outfit was cut way lower than anything she had ever worn before, and she blushed. She turned sideways to look at herself. "This is embarrassing," she said with a sigh.

"It could be worse. At least the skirts are long."

"Yeah. What do you think we should do with our regular uniforms? I have no desire to try and walk over to the Locker Room looking like this."

"I've got an idea—follow me."

Candace followed Glenda back to the picnic area. "Give me your clothes. I think we can stuff them under the table with all the hot dog buns on it, and no one will be the wiser."

Holding both their uniforms, Glenda walked over to the table. She lifted the skirt of the table and thrust their clothes under.

"Done, and now we know where to grab them if we want to make a quick exit," Glenda said.

"I think you're my new hero," Candace said.

"Everyone's got to be one to someone, I guess. Murphy's signaling me. I'll catch you later."

Candace stood for a moment just staring at all the activity. She looked around at the balloons and bunting and wondered again where Tamara was spending her birthday.

She didn't wonder long.

As if by magic, she saw Tamara standing near the stage dressed to kill and larger than life. And in one horrible moment Candace realized that this was Tamara's party and she was there as a servant, not a guest.

Candace wanted nothing more than to turn around and leave. But walking out would be tantamount to quitting her job, and she refused to give Tamara the pleasure.

"Are you okay?" Murphy asked her a moment later.

How could she even begin to answer that question? She couldn't, so instead she asked one of her own. "What do you want me to do?"

"Drinks. I'd like you to keep the punch coming. Take fresh cups to guests who have finished theirs and clear their old cups. There's a tray over by the punch bowl that you can use. Okay?"

"Okay," Candace said.

"You'll be off work at three. I don't know how long the guests will stay, but once it hits three o'clock, you can go home."

"Thank you."

Candace moved over to the punch table and began filling cups and setting them on the tray. She was pretty sure this was not going to go well since she had never tried to actually serve before. Murphy would have been wise to assign the drink task to someone else.

When she had a dozen cups on the tray, she picked it up gingerly, sloshing some of the punch out of the glasses and onto the tray. She carried it carefully to the nearest table and set it down on the edge while still supporting it with her left hand. With her right she passed out drinks.

She made several trips, deliberately leaving Tamara's table for last. When she finally got there, Tamara looked right through her as though she didn't even recognize her. Stunned, Candace sloshed punch all over the table and had to go get napkins to clean it up.

From there, everything became one repetitive nightmare as she frantically struggled to keep up with the punch demand. *How much could these people drink?* she wondered as she scurried from table to table. Perhaps hardest to bear were the puzzled looks she drew from several of Tamara's family members and long-time family friends. She could tell they recognized her but were unclear on why she was there. That was okay; she didn't have the answer to that herself.

Just when she thought it couldn't get any worse, Tamara's younger cousin Trevor, who Candace had babysat a couple of times when he was younger, pinched her. She yelped and spilled her tray down the front of her costume. Several people clapped, which made it all the worse.

She grabbed a fresh uniform and headed for the bathroom to clean up. Once there, she wrestled with the safety pins that Glenda had so carefully placed. She ended up ripping the sleeve slightly and jabbing herself hard in the finger.

She put on the new costume and wrestled again with the safety pins. She left the old uniform soaking in cold water in one of the sinks and walked back to the picnic area, which she was officially renaming the Hell Zone, because surely it was the one place in all the universe where even God wouldn't want to be. When she returned, she believed her suspicions were completely confirmed. They had ended the professional entertainment portion of the program and moved on to karaoke.

16

"This day just keeps getting better and better, doesn't it?" Glenda said as she whizzed by with a tray of hot dogs high above her head.

Candace could only snort a reply as she headed back to the punch table. On stage someone was belting out a horrific rendition of "Open Arms."

She filled her tray with fresh drinks and began distributing them. On her way back to the punch table Glenda walked by again. "Watch out for the kid in the white shirt at the far table. He's grabby."

"I got that," Candace said. "I used to babysit that brat."

"Kids today! No respect."

Her comment was funny since Glenda and Candace were only a couple of years older than him. Unfortunately it wasn't funny enough to cheer her up. She just kept moving, trying to lose herself in the one task she had.

She had half an hour left to go in her shift when someone began singing "I Want Candy." She was going to kill whoever had put that song on the option list. At the same time Tamara walked by her. That was it, Candace couldn't take anymore.

Shifting her full tray to her left hand, she grabbed Tamara's arm with her right.

"We need to talk," Candace said.

Tamara looked like she was going to disagree, but she didn't say anything and she followed Candace over to a bench under some trees. Candace managed to set the tray down without spilling the punch everywhere.

"What is wrong with you?" Candace asked. As soon as the words left her mouth she regretted them. That was no way to start a civilized conversation, but it was the perfect way to start a fight. Before she could apologize, though, Tamara exploded.

"What is wrong with *me*? I'm not the problem here, you are."

"Oh, please. I'm the problem? My dad forced me to get a job. I got a job and suddenly my best friend won't support me or even talk to me? I could have used a little sympathy and commiseration. This is not what I had planned for this summer either."

"Well, you seem to have more fun here than you do with me!"

"Are you crazy? Are you kidding? Oh, that's right. You have no idea how my summer's been going because three days after I started working you stopped answering your phone! You have no idea what I've been through!"

"I'm here now, so tell me," Tamara said, arms crossed.

"I have a boyfriend. My first boyfriend! You weren't there to help me pick out date clothes. You weren't there to talk to when I was freaking out because he's a high school drop-out. You weren't there to tell when we kissed on the Fourth of July and actual fireworks were going off over our heads like in some movie!"

"Oh yeah, your life has been real hard."

"It has because Kurt's ex-girlfriend has it in for me and has been trying to get me fired. She and the guy who tried to run me over with the train are both going to be tied to me by a rope at the end-of-the-summer Scavenger Hunt, and I'm terrified that one of them will finish what they've started. Oh, and let's see, if that isn't bad enough I got randomly drug tested and it came back positive, and I thought I was going to lose my job. They forced me to go home, and you wouldn't answer your phone, and Kurt never once called or came by to see how I was! And the next day when I finally called your house and the maid told me where to find you, I find the two of you together. *And both of you were already avoiding me!* So, I'm sorry if I jumped to some conclusions, but what would you have done? Since I took this job I've been nearly killed, accused of taking drugs, suspended for yelling at a guy who was making lewd comments at me, lost my best friend, have been forced to serve as help at her birthday party where I've been forced to dress in the most humiliating thing I've ever worn, and been pinched by her fifteen-year-old cousin!"

There was silence for a long minute while Candace stood there, panting, fists clenched. Finally Tamara asked, "Trevor pinched you?"

"Yes, the little perv. And because it's my job to be here, I couldn't say or do a thing to him without risking getting fired."

"What happened with the drug test?"

"It turned out to be all the fault of poppy-seed muffins."

"I could have told you that."

"And I wish you would have, but you wouldn't even return my calls, and I needed you," Candace said, beginning to cry.

Tamara stood there, biting her lip. "Do you still need me?" she asked.

"Yes."

"Even though you've got Josh and Kurt and your friends here?"

"Yes. You're my best friend. I'll always need you. And just because I've never really had other friends doesn't make it unreasonable that I find some. I mean, most people have lots of friends. All I've ever had was you. Do you know how that made me feel when you turned your back on me?"

"I'm sorry," Tamara said. "I've been a jerk. I freaked out because I thought you liked this place and these people more than me."

"No, I don't. But I do like some of these people, and despite all of the nightmares, I'm starting to like this place. Can you be okay with that?"

Tamara nodded, starting to cry herself. "As long as I still get to be your best friend."

"Then stop acting like a big dork."

"I can try."

"Okay then."

"Are we good?" Tamara asked.

"I don't know, are we?"

Tamara nodded, and they hugged. Candace was so relieved she started to cry harder.

After a minute they pulled away and they both wiped their eyes. "So, you're going to have to catch me up on Kurt."

"Tonight?" Candace asked.

"Definitely. And you and I will do something cool for my birthday."

"That would be awesome. First, though, I have to do something."

"What?" Tamara asked.

"Come and watch if you like," Candace said, picking up her tray.

Tamara trailed after her as Candace walked back to the party and headed straight for Trevor's table. He was standing up and looking at the stage. Candace walked up to him. "Excuse me, what time is it?"

He glanced at his watch, one that was too expensive for a fifteen-year-old brat like him. "Three oh five, why?"

"That means that I'm officially off the clock. I'm on my own time."

"And?" he asked her with a sleazy smile.

"I just wanted you to know that before I gave you this."

She dumped the entire tray of punch over his head and let it clatter to the ground. Red rivulets ran down his pale hair and stained his shirt and pants. His expression passed from shock to fury as he looked down at himself.

"Have a nice day," Candace said, as cheerily as she could and walked off. Over by the hot-dog table, Glenda gave her the thumbs-up. Candace walked over and picked up her cotton candy uniform from under the table and then left with Tamara.

Tamara and Candace hung out at the Coffee Garden until it closed at midnight, and then headed over to Candace's house for another couple of hours. Since Candace had the next day off, they busily planned a coast drive for Tamara's birthday. It ended up being more of a mall-hopping drive, but they had a great time. Candace told Tamara everything that had been going on at The Zone, while Tamara filled her in on every movie she had missed so far that summer. Tamara didn't even complain when Candace had to go home early to get rested for work the next morning.

Of course, Candace didn't get enough rest that night because once Tamara got home they were up IMing half the night. She barely spoke five words to Becca the next morning when she dropped off Candace's muffin and picked up her cotton candy. Candace dropped the muffin bag on her counter, but before she could put it away, she had actually fallen asleep on her feet.

Candace yelped, startled when a hand fell on her arm, waking her up. She tottered and nearly fell over, but caught herself on the cart. Megan stared at her wide-eyed. Candace was instantly relieved to see that it was Megan and not Lisa who had caught her so unaware.

"Sorry," Megan said.

"No, my bad. What's up?"

"I was just wondering if you would be willing to trade shifts with me on Monday? I work the closing shift, but my friend's playing in a concert and I'd like to go see it."

"Monday, closing shift? Okay, sure."

"Thank you so much! If you ever need to switch shifts, just let me know."

"Okay," Candace said, nodding as she came fully awake. "Do I need to do anything?"

"No, I'll put in the form. Thank you, thank you, thank you!"

"You're welcome."

"I'll leave you to your ... Zoning?"

"Very funny. I like that. See you, Megan."

Candace watched as Megan took off. Just then, she noticed a group of seven referees who seemed to be bearing down on Candace. They were wearing the striped olive green shirts of the Exploration Zone. She looked at their faces and realized none of them looked happy. She turned around to see if there was something behind her that had caught their attention, but there was nothing, just her.

"I'm popular today," she said to herself.

They came to a stop in front of her. One man took an extra step forward, as if designating himself the leader. They all gave her hard looks, and she began to feel like she was some old-time rustler and they were the angry posse.

"Can I help you?" she asked at last.

"You're Candy?" the man out front, Gib by his name tag, asked.

"Yes," she replied, not bothering to correct the shortening of her name.

Everyone began to murmur at that. His eyes focused for a moment on something other than her, and he took a quick step forward and snatched the Muffin Mansion bag off her cart.

"Care to explain this?" he asked.

Candace crossed her arms. "Why should I?" she asked.

"It's just that I've never seen you in the Muffin Mansion," he said. "I think I'd remember seeing a cotton candy operator in there."

Once again, the group behind him began to murmur, and several bobbed their heads up and down.

"It's true, I've never been in there," she said.

"Then how did you come to be in possession of this?" he asked, waving the bag under her nose. "And don't bother lying, because we already know the truth."

The group parted down the middle to reveal a woman in the back, about ten years older than Candace. Her hair was falling down from a bun at the back of her head. There were several fresh scratches covering her face, and her shirt had been torn. In her hands were the remnants of a cotton candy stick. It was squashed and torn in places, and one long tendril of spun sugar swung free and hung down to her knees.

"I got it from Becca."

"And in exchange?" Gib prompted.

She tried desperately to figure out what he was getting at, even as she couldn't take her eyes off the woman holding the crushed cone. "I gave her cotton candy."

The whole group lurched forward a step at that, causing Candace to hastily retreat farther behind her cart.

Gib's eyes were blazing and he fixed her with his glare. "Becca is allergic to sugar. It makes her hyper and a little bit crazy. Everybody in this park knows not to give her any. Especially not cotton candy, which is her favorite."

"We've suspected for the last couple of weeks," the woman in the back said, eyes wide and frightened-looking. "We couldn't prove it, though."

"She was starting to get that little extra bounce to her step," another man spoke up.

"And yesterday we caught her hopping. Hopping, hopping, always hopping," another spoke up.

"And then we knew," Gib said. "So we laid a trap and we caught her. Poor Ruth there took the brunt of it."

The woman with the cotton candy nodded miserably.

"What have you done to Becca?" Candace whispered.

"I wouldn't worry about her. I would concern yourself with what we'll do to you if you ever give her cotton candy again," Gib said, his voice low and threatening.

They all took a step closer just as Candace found her panic button and pushed it. To her dismay when the security guard arrived seconds later, he was alone. His eyes swept her and the angry group facing her, and his hand went to his radio. Apparently even the security guards had panic buttons.

He stepped over so that he was standing next to Candace. His eyes flitted back and forth seeming to take in everything. Finally he turned to her. "You didn't give Becca sugar, did you?"

And suddenly, he was no longer standing beside her, her rescuer, but rather standing with her accusers.

"I didn't know!" she wailed. "Nobody told me."

"You mean you would have us believe that nobody told you to watch out for Becca?" Gib asked.

"People told me that, but they never told me what that meant. And then when I met her she was really nice."

"And you never once thought to ask?"

"I—"

At that moment the rest of the cavalry arrived. There were fifteen guards surrounding them all in a circle, each bigger and tougher looking than the last.

"No, okay, I never asked why people told me to watch out for Becca. I've been kind of busy with problems of my own. I know now, thank you, I won't give her any more cotton candy. Okay?"

Gib stared at her through squinted eyes as if trying to measure her up. Finally he asked, "Do we have your word on that?"

"Yes, you do. No more cotton candy for Becca."

He nodded as though satisfied, and just like that the stand-off was over. The group moved away, along with most of the security guards. The lead guard, though, stepped close to Candace. "You actually gave Becca cotton candy?" he asked.

"Yes."

"You realize that that's like dumping blood into shark-infested waters before going in for a swim, right?"

"How was I suppose to know? She seemed so nice!"

"She is nice. Sweetest thing in the world, except when it comes to sugar. She's going to be back looking for more. You see her, hit the button and we'll come help."

Candace shook her head. This was all ridiculous. "Seriously, how much trouble can she be?"

"Last year during Scavenger Hunt, she got into a jar of Jelly Bellies and began to run amok. It took five of us to bring her down."

"You're kidding!"

"Wish I was. I've still got the scars to prove it," he said ruefully before walking off.

"Insane," Candace muttered to herself as she watched him go. "Everyone who works here is completely insane. And I will be too if I don't get out of here soon."

17

Candace had the house to herself for the weekend when her parents decided to take a spontaneous trip. They left Saturday and weren't due back until Tuesday. Tamara and Candace spent most of the weekend catching up and even caught a matinee early Monday before Candace had to go to work—thanks to taking Megan's closing shift. To celebrate her first time having to work closing, Kurt was taking her out to dinner afterwards.

It only took Candace one night to discover that she didn't like working the closing shift. During the height of summer, The Zone closed at midnight on weekends and eleven on weeknights. The food carts were open half an hour later so people could grab their last snack on the way out of the park. Then she had to walk her cart to its area behind the Exploration Zone where it was stored. Since it was Monday, she wouldn't be off work until about ten minutes to midnight. The good news was Denny's was always open.

Everything was going according to plan until it was time to walk the cart to storage. The time came and went, and the cart didn't move. She walked all around it, trying to figure out what was wrong. In the mornings the cart started on its own, and she walked beside it as it left storage. She had assumed that it would do the same when it was time to shut down. It was quiet, though, and the motor never started its whirring. Finally she managed to get the intercom working.

"Um, yeah, this is Candace with cart five, and we're not moving anywhere."

"Candace, hold on and someone will come to you," a voice came back.

"Okay, great," she said.

She waited, glancing around the park. All the players had finally gone, and the last of the referees waved to her as they walked to the exit. She had been in the park before opening, but there was always a lot of hustle and bustle. Cleaning and maintenance crews worked from six until the park opened, and refs were always milling about.

Now, though, everything seemed so barren. It gave her the creeps. She glanced at her watch. It was twelve fifteen. She was already fifteen minutes late to meet Kurt in the Locker Room.

"Come on, hurry up, I'm starving," she complained, as though that would somehow speed someone her way. After another five minutes had passed, she used the intercom again.

"Hello, this is Candace with cart five, and we're still waiting over here in The Extreme Zone."

This time there was no answer. "Hello?" she tried again. "Hello? Anyone listening? If so, this isn't funny. I'd like to get out of here."

Only silence greeted her.

Great, now what am I supposed to do? Can I just leave the cart here? Maybe it will still be here when I get back in just a few hours. Or maybe it will have fixed itself by then, or they'll finally have gotten someone over here to take a look at it.

She looked around and realized that now, not only could she not see anybody else, but she couldn't hear anything either. During the day there was always so much noise from people laughing, talking, and screaming on the rides. Then there was the background music and the noise of the rides themselves. Now there was nothing, just silence.

"Okay, this is getting creepy."

Suddenly she saw a lone figure approaching, and she waved. "Over here. The cart is broken."

"Candace? You okay?"

She recognized Kurt's voice with relief.

"I'm fine, but the cart's broken. They said they were sending someone to fix it. That was several minutes ago, though, and now no one's answering on the radio."

"I got worried when you didn't show. I came to see if you were okay."

"Thank you," she said. "What do you think I should do? Should I leave it?"

"Let me see if I can go find someone," Kurt said. "I'll be right back."

"Hurry," she said.

It seemed like forever, but it was only about ten minutes before he returned. He had a strained look on his face.

"We've got a little problem."

"They're not coming to fix the cart?" she asked.

"Um. It's a bit bigger problem."

"What?"

"It looks like we're the only two people here and we're locked in."

She burst out laughing. "That's a good one."

"Not kidding. Really locked in."

"Okay. Not laughing. Are you sure?"

"Yeah, pretty sure."

She left the cart and headed for the cast exit at a run. Kurt ran beside her. When she got there she saw that the gates were all closed and padlocked shut. She shook one experimentally, but it didn't budge. She took off and headed for the front of the park where she checked both the exit gate and the entrance turnstiles. Everything was locked up tight with gates across them.

That only left the emergency exit at the back of the park. She ran there too, afraid of what she'd find.

"Locked! All of them!" she cried, shaking the gate that stood between her and freedom. "We're totally trapped."

"Looks like it," he said.

"There's got to be some way out," she said. "Someone we can call."

"I don't know. Mascots never work closing shifts."

"Do you have your cell phone at least?"

He shook his head. "I left it charging in the car."

"Mine's in the Locker Room." Kurt followed her as she ran there next. The door was closed, and when she grabbed it, she found that it, too, was locked.

"How could they lock the Locker Room?"

"Probably for security. Lots of people leave stuff in there permanently. If you've got an idea of who we can call, we can use one of the pay phones and call collect."

"My parents are out of town. What about yours?"

"They live like five hours away. I room with four other mascots who were all going to some party tonight."

"No help there. We could call the police."

"And tell them what? We're stuck in the theme park? I'm not sure they'd have any better idea of who to call than we would."

A thought occurred to her. "Do you have Josh's number memorized?"

"No."

That left only Tamara. Surely she could help her figure a way out of the park. They went to the nearest pay phone and Candace called her collect.

"Why on earth are you calling me collect?" Tamara asked, sounding tired and bewildered.

"Because I can't get to my phone. I need help. I'm locked inside The Zone."

"Oh my! You're all by yourself?"

"No, Kurt's with me. It's just the two of us, and we've tried every exit."

"You're trapped inside the theme park with Kurt," Tamara said, sounding instantly more awake.

"Yes."

"Candace, I know I've been a bad friend all summer. But I'm going to make that all up to you right now."

"Thank you," Candace said, relief flooding through her.

"I'll tell you what I'm going to do."

"Yes?"

"I'm going to hang up the phone and go back to sleep."

"What?"

"You're trapped somewhere cool with the guy you're crazy about. There's nothing more romantic than that. Trust me, you'll thank me later. Call me in the morning when you get out and tell me all about it."

There was a click as Tamara hung up the phone. Candace just stood for a moment, staring at the receiver in her hand before hanging it up. "She's not going to help," she said.

"I heard," Kurt said, sounding strangled.

She turned and saw that he was laughing. She punched him in the arm, but it didn't stop him. "How can you be laughing?"

"I just realized. Whenever I came here as a kid I fantasized about all the things I would do if I could manage to hide out until the park was closed. I would make a game out of figuring out where I would sleep—the whole thing. And now's it actually happened, and all we can think of is how to get out."

He laughed harder, and after a minute Candace joined in. He was right. They were living the dream of thousands, maybe millions. They made movies about this sort of thing—spending the night in stores, museums, train stations. What better place than a theme park?

"Well, if you don't mind pure sugar, I know where we can get something to eat," she said, pointing in the direction of her broken-down cart.

They actually managed to do a little better than that. Over where the carts were stored they discovered that whoever ran the beef jerky cart had neglected to lock the food storage bin properly. They dined on beef jerky and cotton candy and washed it all down with water from one of the water fountains.

With a full stomach, things began to look up for Candace. Now that she wasn't alone, the silence of the park also seemed magical. It was like an entirely different world where giant monsters slept and darkened buildings lay waiting for their treasures to be discovered.

Kurt took her on a full guided tour of the History Zone, pointing out things that she had never noticed or never fully appreciated the significance of.

"Do you know how many chairs there are in Poor Richard's Pub?" he asked.

"No."

"Fifty-six. One for each signer of the Declaration of Independence."

"That's cool."

"Yeah, history is awesome. Especially here in The Zone where they blur the lines between fact and fantasy."

They sat down on a bench facing the carousel. She could totally see Kurt teaching history to kids. He clearly had a passion for the subject. She wondered if he had ever thought about it. It would give him something to strive for, certainly something to go back to school for.

"Am I boring you?" he asked, suddenly.

"No, no. I like hearing you talk."

"Yeah, but you're thinking about something else. What is it?"

"Well, history is cool and everything," she said. "I guess I just spend more time thinking about the future."

"Oh, like what's going to happen to the human race? Global warming and space travel and is there life out there?"

"No, not that, I mean *my* future. Where I'm going to college, what kind of career I'm going to have, that sort of stuff."

"Oh. You know, I try not to think about that kind of stuff. Live in the moment, that's what I say."

"That's nice, but don't you need to have a sense of where you're going?" she prompted.

"Nope."

"But don't you ever think about what you're going to do next year or next month?"

"I try not to even think about next week," he said with a laugh. "Why would I? I like my job, I'm dating a cute girl, everything's great."

Her heart began to pound when he called her cute, but she forced her thoughts away from that. "But, you can't work at The Zone for the rest of your life."

"I don't know. Someday maybe I'll figure something else out, but until that day comes, why bother?"

His answer irritated her. He had so much potential, but he seemed content just to waste it. "So that you'll be prepared," Candace said, louder than she had intended. "We're not kids forever. I may not know what I want to do with my life yet, but I know I want to do something. The whole world is out there, and I want to see more than just Rivervale. Sooner or later you have to take responsibility for your own life, and I'm trying. What are you doing? You couldn't even commit to finishing high school."

There, it was out. All her misgivings—all her fears about him—shimmered in the air between them. She took a deep breath, afraid of what he was going to say.

"What do you want, Candace?" he asked.

There were so many ways to answer that. She wanted to be valued, respected, taken seriously. She wanted to really live and grow. She wanted to share all of that with someone. "I want a guy who values the same things I do," she said after a moment. It was the truth. A Christian guy who valued what she did would take her seriously, would help her grow as a person, and would love and respect her. She wanted—needed—Kurt to be that guy.

"Then you're going to have to find some other guy, because I'm not him," Kurt said, his voice cold and distant.

She nodded. She had backed him into a corner, and she shouldn't have expected anything else. She stood up slowly. "Then I guess there's nothing else to say."

He wouldn't look at her. He just sat, staring off into the distance with his jaw clenched. He shook his head but didn't say anything.

"Okay," Candace said, and she walked off.

Earlier with Kurt the empty park had seemed like a magical place, but now it felt like a ghost town, haunted by memories and silent as the grave. She walked through the Exploration Zone, and The Atomic Coaster reared up against the dark sky, cold and unfeeling.

She kept walking until she reached the Splash Zone. There the sounds of swiftly moving water broke the silence and comforted her. Josh had once told her that they kept the water circulating in all the rides, even at night, so that it didn't grow stagnant. She found a bench and sat down, closed her eyes, and let the sounds wash over her.

She was changing. She could feel it. Day by day for the last several weeks she had been changing just a bit at a time so it took a while to notice. At the beginning of the summer she would have been content to let Kurt be as he was, and his lack of ambition about his future would not have bothered her. The changes in herself also caused a lot of friction between her and Tamara. At the beginning of the summer Tamara was her only close friend, and now she had others who she also confided in, like Josh. Once she would have been content to let Tamara pay for everything for the rest of their lives, but that had changed too. Candace wanted to make her own way in the world. She wanted a future and a goal, and neither Kurt nor Tamara seemed to understand that. At least she knew she could eventually get Tamara to respect her wishes, but Kurt was a different story.

She tried to tell herself she just wanted what was best for him, that she was looking out for his good, but in reality she was looking out for what was best for her. She liked Kurt, a lot, and she wanted to continue dating him for a long, long time. She knew, though, that they were not walking the same path in life, and unless that changed there was no future with him.

"When did I become so grown up?" she asked out loud.

The water seemed to murmur an answer that she couldn't quite understand. What was it Martha had said? *Never date a guy you ain't willing to marry.* It was good advice, even if it had seemed much too grim when she had first heard it. Candace wished she could talk to Martha just then. She thought about calling Tamara back but decided against it. There would be enough to talk about later. There were only a few hours left of the night anyway, and soon she would be free. It seemed Candace had regained her best friend only just in time to help her cope with losing her boyfriend.

18

After sitting and listening to the soothing sounds of the water for about an hour, curiosity overcame Candace. The park was very dark, but her eyes had adjusted somewhat. When would she ever have a chance like this again? She had the park nearly to herself, so now was the time to do some exploration.

She wandered around for a few minutes, poking her head in various places before inspiration struck. She hurried to the Kids Zone and approached the Little Red Riding Hood ride. She was able to climb over the railing and then walk next to the tracks through the ride. She stopped to peek around characters and scenes. The tinny music was absent, and nothing was moving in the ride. It was cool and weird at the same time. She finally came to a good scene inside the Grandmother's cottage, and she walked over and touched the bed gingerly.

It seemed real enough. Feeling completely naughty, she sat down on it slowly. It supported her weight. She lay down on it and started pretending to be the wolf. "The better to eat you with!" she finished with a growl. The figure of Red was standing close by with a surprised look on her face, and Candace laughed.

"Yes, this is definitely where I would live if I lived in the park. My own little cottage with a comfy bed."

Too comfy, she realized as her mind started to drift. She sat up abruptly. It would be bad to fall asleep and be found here in the morning. She got up quickly and made sure to straighten the flowery quilt.

Whew, that could have been embarrassing, she realized as she continued walking through the ride to the exit. Once outside, she debated briefly where to go next until inspiration struck again.

Minutes later she was in the Game Zone. Rows of games of skill and chance stood silent. She herself had claimed a few of the stuffed animal prizes over the years. There was one game, though, that had always taunted her. One game she believed impossible to win.

She walked past several games until she stood before the ring toss. The idea was simple enough: toss a plastic ring and have it land around the neck of one of the hundreds of glass bottles sitting wedged together in a square. So simple, yet so utterly impossible. The giant stuffed dogs hanging from the ceiling of the game mocked her. She'd tried before to win one. She had seen an occasional person walking through the park carrying one, but deep down she was sure they must be ringers, bringing false hope and taunting people with the thought that it must be possible to win.

Candace hopped over the counter and scooped herself up several bucketfuls of plastic rings. When she had a large number, she hopped back over the counter. It was one of the few areas of the park that seemed to have some low emergency lights on, and the moon had begun to shine brightly, glinting off some of the bottles.

She went through more than a hundred rings, and none of them found their mark. Finally, she picked up a bucket and tossed the entire contents at the bottles. There was a hail of sharp pings as rings hit and bounced crazily off the glass bottles. When all the rings had landed, she saw that one bottle had a ring around its neck. A shaft of moonlight illuminated it and she stood in awe, staring. It was as though God was shining the light down just for her, trying to get her attention, trying to get her to talk to him.

She sat down on the counter, leaned her back against the corner pillar, and began to pray.

"God, I'm so tired and confused," she said, whispering the words out loud. "I like Kurt so much, but we are different and I know he thinks I'm trying to change him. God, I just wish he could open his eyes and see his own future, his own potential." Tears started to roll down her cheeks. "It's been a terrible summer and a wonderful summer, and so much is changing in my life that I feel so lost. Please, help me. I get upset at Kurt, but I'm just as bad as he is. I don't know what I want out of life. It's like I've always believed that somehow there would be a giant neon sign in the sky saying 'Candace, do this.' Well, there isn't."

She opened her eyes for a moment and stared at the shaft of moonlight which was moving slowly from the bottle with the ring around it toward the counter on which she was sitting. She smiled and closed her eyes again. "At least, I don't think there is. It's hard to imagine that in a few months I'll be applying for colleges and trying to pick a major. How do you pick a direction when you just don't know? God, help me to find the place where I belong in this world."

A few minutes later she fell asleep.

"Candace!"

She woke, hearing someone call her name. She opened her eyes to find that it was much lighter out. A janitor was staring at her, an amused expression on his face. She was still sitting on the counter, and she felt stiff all over.

"You okay?" he asked.

"Yes, I think so. We got locked in."

"We know. When we showed up this morning to unlock everything we found Kurt. He told us what happened to you two. He didn't know where you were, so we've been looking for you."

"I'm so sorry to be so much trouble. My cart?" she asked, thinking about it.

"We've got a maintenance guy over there fixing it. We're still not sure why no one came to get you last night. Some mix-up, no doubt. We called your supervisor, and she said for you to go home. You can make up for today by working on Friday instead."

"Thank you," Candace said, very grateful to have other people taking care of everything. She stood slowly, trying to stretch out the kinks. "Is the Locker Room open?"

"Yup, you can get your stuff."

"Awesome," she said with a yawn. She started to go.

He gestured toward the bottles and she stopped, puzzled. "Did you get that ring around the bottle?"

"Yes."

"Were you standing where you're supposed to? You didn't just drop it there?"

"No, I was standing outside. I went through ten buckets."

"Well, then, why are you leaving without your prize?" he asked, reaching up and unhooking one of the big dogs from the ceiling.

"But, I didn't pay to play," she said.

He looked her over, and she was suddenly aware of her bedraggled, disheveled appearance. "Oh, I think you did," he said. "If you feel too bad about it, you can always come by later and throw some more money away trying to get one of these things. It's nearly impossible, you know."

He handed her the big dog that was at least four feet tall. "It took a miracle," she admitted. "Thank you," she told the man.

He gave her a brief salute, and she took the dog—which she decided to name Happy—to the Locker Room where she rescued her stuff. She made it to the car, settled Happy in the passenger seat, flipped open her phone, and called Tamara, waking her.

"So, how did it go?" Tamara asked. "Was it wonderful? Was it romantic?"

"We broke up," Candace said shortly.

"Oh."

"Take me out to breakfast and I'll tell you all about it."

"Deal."

Candace drove to Tamara's. Tamara stared incredulously as Candace hauled Happy into the house with her. "Can he stay here while we're out at breakfast?" Candace asked. "I don't want to leave him in the car."

"That depends. Is he house trained?"

"Does it matter?" Candace asked, too tired to come up with something witty to say.

"No. Let's go get you some food."

"I have to work Friday to make up for the fact that I'm not working today," Candace said, hoping Tamara would understand.

"That's okay," Tamara said, "I'm overdue to see that Glider ride you told me all about."

A few minutes later Candace was tearing into a huge chicken, cheese, and onion omelet. She hadn't realized just how hungry she was until the waitress set the plate in front of her.

"I take it dinner last night was less than stellar," Tamara said.

"Beef jerky and cotton candy."

"By the time the summer is over you won't want to eat cotton candy ever again."

"Or smell it."

Tamara wrinkled her nose in distaste. "So, what happened with you and Kurt?"

Candace shook her head. "Everything was fine. We were walking around the History Zone and he was telling me all about it. Before I knew it we were talking about the future and I basically accused him of being a total slacker."

"Ouch. I'm guessing that didn't go over so well."

"Good guess. I mean, the weirdest part is that he's a smart guy. He could totally be a history teacher or something."

Tamara shrugged. "You never know. Maybe his parents put too much pressure on him and he just doesn't want to deal for a while."

"That's the other thing I found out. His parents live hours and hours away. He shares a house with a bunch of other guys."

"Well, he is over eighteen. He can do that," Tamara said.

"Whose side are you on?" Candace asked.

"Yours. I'm just trying to maybe help you see things a little more objectively."

"I think it might be a little late for that," Candace said glumly. "He was pretty upset. I don't know. Maybe it's for the best. I mean, where could this relationship really have gone?"

Tamara shook her head. "I don't know. If you want to get him back, though, it's probably not too late."

Candace sighed. "I can't even think about that at the moment."

"You look thrashed. You need some sleep."

"I had a little bit. I think that's part of the problem. It's easier to pull an all-nighter than it is to get like two hours of sleep. Next time I'm going to stay in Grandma's house."

"Huh?"

"The Little Red Riding Hood ride," Candace said, stifling a yawn. "Grandma has a comfy bed."

"If you say so."

When Candace returned to work on Wednesday, she discovered that the tale of her and Kurt being trapped in the park had grown to epic proportions, complete with a crazed murderer who stalked them all over the park with a butcher knife.

"What?" Candace asked in disbelief as Josh related the tale.

He nodded. "It's pretty heroic. Everyone thinks you came close to being toasted."

"That's ridiculous. Nothing even remotely like that happened."

"Good luck explaining that. People will just think you're being modest."

She was totally amazed. "Was I at least cool and not some helpless wimpy girl?"

"You kicked butt. If it weren't for you, the police wouldn't have caught the guy."

"What police?"

"The ones who made a daring rescue attempt just before dawn, storming the front gates of the park."

"That's just crazy."

Josh shrugged. "Every urban legend begins somewhere. Just wait, you'll see. There's already buzz that they're going to find some way to incorporate it into one of the Halloween mazes."

"But none of that happened!"

"Doesn't matter. By next summer, it will be a fact as far as anyone knows."

"This is too weird," Candace said, feeling a headache starting.

He laughed. "Just think, someday when you bring your kids here and they find out that it was you, you'll be a total hero to them."

"I'd hope I could be a hero to my kids for something I actually did rather than something people said I did."

When Lisa came to give her a break, Candace noticed that the other girl looked smug. *She probably heard that Kurt and I broke up*, Candace thought.

Sure enough, Lisa said, "Candace, so sorry to hear about you and Kurt. You really hurt his feelings. I'm just glad I could be there to give him a ... shoulder ... to cry on."

Candace wanted to punch her. Worse, since Lisa knew what had actually happened, that meant she had to have gotten it from the horse's mouth. After all, the stories of adventure and murderers didn't say anything about a messy breakup. "Get out of here, Lisa."

"But I'm here to give you your break."

"I don't need one right now, thank you. Now leave."

Lisa strutted away.

"Sorry," Josh said. "I hadn't heard."

"It's okay," Candace said.

"What happened?"

"I don't really want to talk about it," Candace sighed.

"Cool enough."

"Tell me again how I stopped the murderer and saved the day?"

He laughed and went over the whole story again in detail, this time adding his own little flourishes. The story became so much more outrageous than even the first telling that Candace finally had to laugh. Fixating on the outrageous tale helped her to stop thinking quite so much about Kurt and about the look of triumph she had seen in Lisa's eyes.

19

A week before the great Scavenger Hunt, the entire mood at the park seemed to change. The players, especially the younger ones, stayed later and played harder, as though they could sense summer drawing to an end. Among the referees there was a spirit of restlessness, as of a great change coming that they all were preparing for. In California, the seasons of the year were not nearly as pronounced as they were in most of the rest of the country. At The Zone, though, the seasons were clearly regulated, and soon it would be fall.

Candace's time at the park was coming to an end. She wasn't nearly as excited as she had expected to be. She found herself watching some of the year-round referees wistfully. Each of them seemed to be vibrating with a new energy. What would it like to be there for all the events of the coming months?

Candace finally asked Martha about it. The older woman smiled at the question. "Summer is everyone's least favorite season to work. It's too crowded, too hot, and too monotonous. What you're sensing is the anticipation all us old-timers feel when summer draws to a close and we can start to prepare for autumn."

It made sense. She, herself, was starting to feel anticipation for returning to school. It was her senior year, and she intended to make the most of it.

In addition to the end of summer chaos, there was a steadily building frenzy revolving around the Scavenger Hunt. More teams could be seen every day in the park doing practice runs and team-building exercises. Josh's team members had taken to holding up signs that said We Want Pizza! as they passed by her cart.

"What is that about?" Sue asked one day, seeing one of the signs go by while she was using her break to chat with Candace.

"I bet Josh that the loser would buy the other's team pizza."

Sue looked serious for a moment. "You didn't involve all of us in that, did you?"

"No, just me. If we lose, I buy them all pizza."

Sue looked relieved. "And if we win?"

"Josh buys all of us pizza."

"Well, then, let's plan to trash them."

"I just don't know how. They've got it all together, and our team will be lucky not to fall down on the railroad tracks and get run over."

"You've heard of David and Goliath. Where there's a will, God has a way."

"I like that," Candace said, laughing.

"Feel free to use it," Sue said. "See you later."

"Later."

Candace was once again in the Splash Zone, but she hadn't seen Josh all day. She knew he was scheduled to work, so she wondered if he was okay. When her shift was finally done for the day, he appeared, as if by magic.

"Where have you been?" she asked.

"Special project. Come with me. I want to show you something," he said, grabbing her hand and pulling her with him.

"Where are we going?" she asked, jogging to keep up.

"Somewhere."

"What's going on?" Candace asked.

"It's a surprise," Josh said.

She let him lead her all the way across the park. Finally they arrived at the picnic area where Tamara had had her birthday party. It looked like there was some party going on. People were milling all around. There were several guys in suits and a lot of refs.

On the platform reserved for entertainment stood several people, and she suddenly recognized one of them.

"Wait, is that—"

"The owner of the park, former quarterback John Hanson? Yup."

"What is going on?" she asked.

"See for yourself."

Josh cleared his throat and then spoke loudly, "She's here."

Suddenly all faces were turned toward Candace, and people were cheering and clapping. "There's got to be some mistake," she said to Josh.

"Nope, no mistake."

John Hanson spoke loudly into the microphone, "Come on up here, Candace!"

Trembling, she made her way toward the stage. When she reached the edge, he leaned down and offered her his hand to help her up. He then showed her to a seat.

"Ladies and gentlemen. I want to take this opportunity to thank all of you for coming out today. It's truly a great occasion."

There was applause, and Candace sat on her chair, staring at John Hanson's back. In front of him a sea of people were gathered, listening to his every word with rapt attention. *What was she doing here?*

"It isn't every day that you get to take something you've built and make it better. For quite a while there's been a team of people brainstorming how to attract more corporate and private events to The Zone. And now, thanks, to the little lady behind me, we have the solution!"

There was more applause as Candace sat there, desperately trying to figure out what was going on.

"And so, I give you the new and improved Party Zone!"

The crowd roared as huge bags of confetti exploded and rained down on everyone. Candace reached out her hand and caught several pieces—pink and green and blue.

"And now, let's hear from Candace, the referee who gave this place its new name."

Candace shook her head wildly, but John hauled her to her feet and dragged her toward the microphone. "Speech!" people in the crowd began shouting.

It was like a scene straight out of one of her nightmares, with the exception that she wasn't standing in her underwear. She glanced down quickly just to make sure.

"I don't know what to say," she spoke into the microphone. "I mean, I don't know, somehow the name seemed like a no-brainer to me."

A roar of laughter greeted that.

"What can I say, really? This is the strangest day yet in the weirdest, coolest summer of my life," she said.

The crowd laughed. "I mean, half the time I can't even seem to get my cotton candy cart to do what I want." More laughter followed.

"So, I guess I'd just like to thank all of you for helping me out and being so nice. Thank you."

She tried to retreat back to her seat, but John caught her hand. "Hold on, there's one more thing left to do," he said.

Candace just stared, barely believing what was happening. Suddenly he handed her a pair of giant scissors. She grasped them awkwardly.

"And now, my dear, if you would be so kind as to cut the ribbon and declare this Party Zone open for business," he said, maneuvering her over to the side of the stage where a big red ribbon was strung.

She swung the scissors around and brought them to bear on the ribbon, and with a snip the ribbon dropped to the ground.

The crowd cheered its approval, and Candace seriously considered fainting. John took the scissors from her and whispered, "You can leave now if you like."

She nodded and hopped off the stage with the help of Josh. "That was awesome!" he told her.

She punched him in the shoulder. "Is this your doing?"

"Nope, you've got your supervisor to thank for that."

"Great. Can you just get me out of here?" she asked.

He nodded and led the way through the press of the crowd. From the looks of things, half the players were in attendance along with every ref not actively working.

They made it through finally, and Josh walked her toward the Locker Room. Out in the clear she began to breathe easier.

"Trust me," he said, "this falls under the category of days you'll look back on and cherish."

"Right now it's just falling under the category of bizarre. Thanks for helping me get out of there."

"Hey, that's what friends do, right? They keep each other's secrets and help each other out."

"I guess so."

"And speaking of secrets, I think you owe me a new one. The old one's kinda outdated," he said.

"It's a deal."

"Candace!" Candace spun around to see Tamara rushing after her. "You were awesome!" her friend said, cheeks flushed and out of breath.

"Thanks. I felt like an idiot. I didn't even know all that was going to happen," Candace said, hugging Tamara. "Wait a minute, how come you're here?"

"A little bird told me," Tamara said with a laugh. "That was so cool."

Suddenly Candace realized that she had totally forgotten her manners. "Oh, I'm sorry. Tamara, this is my friend, Josh. Josh, this is my best friend, Tamara."

They shook hands. "So what do we do now?" Tamara asked, eyes wide.

"Well, I'm off work," Candace said. "I'd just like to get out of here."

"Cool. Ice cream?"

"You read my mind."

"I'll catch you ladies later," Josh said.

"Wait, I thought you could come with us," Tamara said.

He grinned. "Stellar. Come on, Candace, let's grab our stuff so we can get out of here."

"Meet me out front," Tamara said. "I'll drive."

Josh turned and headed toward the Locker Room. Candace lingered for a minute. "Are you sure?" she asked Tamara in a whisper.

"I've been enough of a pain about you having other friends. I think it's time I get to know them."

Candace gave Tamara a quick hug and then raced after Josh.

"Tamara seems cool," Josh said as he and Candace walked toward the front of the park.

"She's great," Candace said. She glanced sideways at Josh, wishing she could read him better. "You know, she's not seeing anybody. You could ask her out if you wanted to."

He shook his head. "She seems like a rich girl."

"So?"

"I don't date rich girls."

"Why?"

"They're usually not very down to earth. Don't get me wrong, Tamara seems nice, not snobby or anything, but still."

"She does think that she can buy anything, even if it's not for sale," Candace joked.

"I knew it! Yeah, she seems cool, but just not my type."

Candace wasn't so sure. It had seemed for a moment when the two shook hands that there had been some sort of spark. Maybe she was imagining it. Still, it was no stranger than anything else that day.

When they left Big D's an hour later, all three of them were sticky with ice cream. To be fair, although Josh had started the ice-cream fight that had gotten the three of them kicked out of the restaurant, neither she nor Tamara had hesitated to hurl ice cream back at him.

Tamara dropped them both back at The Zone to get their cars, and then Candace headed straight home to get a shower and throw her uniform in the wash. As soon as she got out of the shower, she saw that Tamara had IMd her.

U there?

   Yeah.

That was totally fun. ☺

   It took me 30 min to wash ice cream out of my hair,

Candace typed.

Ha! Only took me 20.

   Thanks. I had fun.

Me too. Josh is pretty cool.

   Yeah, lots of fun.

And way hot.

Candace laughed.

Someone crushing?

   No, just admiring. Not my type.

Candace sat back and stared at that for a moment. Finally she responded.

   Does that matter?

Don't know. I think so. Sorry I didn't get to know him sooner.

Yeah, summer could have been a lot more fun.

At least it's fun now. ☺

U said it.

So, what are we going to do tomorrow night?

I don't know. We could take Josh to the Coffee Garden and try to get kicked out of there.

LOL!!

TTFN

Hasta la bye bye.

20

For the next couple of days every ref that passed Candace went out of their way to high-five her and congratulate her. It was like she was a celebrity. As Scavenger Hunt got closer, though, everyone became preoccupied with it again. Even Candace was getting excited, and the night before she could barely sleep.

The day of Scavenger Hunt dawned, and she had arrived at work with butterflies in her stomach. The event didn't start until after dark but the anticipation that filled the Locker Room was overwhelming. Teams had posted signs everywhere naming and proclaiming themselves champions. Of course, the one sign that was larger than all the others simply read: We Want Pizza!

"Candace, I've got a special project for you today," Martha said, approaching Candace as soon as she exited the Locker Room.

"What?" Candace asked suspiciously. "Last time you had a special thing for me to do, it directly resulted in me ending up on stage and having to give a speech."

"Yes, but aren't you glad? And the Party Zone is a much better name than the picnic area. Already bookings have tripled, I hear. People are excited, and it has breathed new life into the area."

Candace rolled her eyes. "What do you want me to do?"

"I need you to make some cotton candy and package it for one of our stadium events."

"You mean put it in those plastic bags?"

"Exactly."

"Oh, that doesn't sound so bad," Candace admitted.

"You'll be working off field and in the shade."

"I am totally your girl," Candace said.

Martha smiled. "I thought you might be. We're going to need quite a lot of it, so I requisitioned you some help."

Candace followed Martha over to her cart, which was parked under some shade trees behind a building. Beside it there were several cardboard boxes filled with cones. Another large box was filled with plastic sleeves and twist ties. Yet another box had cardboard flats that were designed to hold the finished cotton candies. Candace's eyes bugged out of her head.

"That's a lot of cotton candy," she said.

"Yes, it is."

"Hi, Candace," Sue said, joining them.

"I couldn't pull anyone off carts, so I was able to get Sue here to help you."

"Just tell me what to do," Sue said.

"Okay, this is going to take a while," Candace said.

"I have absolute faith in you ladies. Call me on the walkie-talkie if you need anything," Martha said as she walked away.

"Wow," Candace said.

"What part do you want me to do?" Sue asked.

"Well, if you could handle putting the cotton candy in the plastic bag and stacking them in those cardboard holders, that would be great," Candace said.

"Consider it done."

"This is not how I envisioned spending my day," Candace said, picking up the first empty cone and stepping toward the machine.

"Me either," Sue laughed. "But you won't hear me complaining."

It took about fifteen minutes to establish a groove. Soon they were ripping along faster than Candace would have thought possible. Because of the size of the bags, she had to put less cotton candy on the sticks than she was used to, but that helped everything move faster.

After a couple of hours they had managed to go through nearly half the boxes of cones and several vats of cotton candy. Candace's wrists and back were starting to ache from the constant motion.

"Since we seem to be all alone on this, I think it's up to us to call our own breaks," Candace said.

"Works for me," Sue answered.

Candace picked up the walkie-talkie and contacted Martha, who confirmed that they could break whenever they needed to.

"Sounds like she was pleased with our progress," Sue noted.

"I hope so, because I'm not sure I can keep it up," Candace said.

"Don't forget we have a half day today. If we don't finish, someone else will have to ... unless it can wait until tomorrow," Sue said.

"That's right, I had forgotten about that," Candace said.

It was Scavenger Hunt day, and to keep from having some referees tired after working full days competing against referees who had had the day off, everyone was supposed to work a half day. That way, theoretically, it was all fair.

"I'm getting pretty excited," Sue admitted. "What do you think it will be like?"

"Well, I've talked to a couple of people who've done it before, and it sounds like a cross between a traditional scavenger hunt and a trivia contest," Candace said. "We'll have to run all over the park looking for things and writing things down on a piece of paper."

"Someone should probably bring a flashlight, then."

"I hadn't thought of that, but that's a really good idea. Even if they have all the lights on, who knows what we're going to be trying to find."

"And if they don't have all the lights on, it will be wicked dark."

Candace shook her head. "Tell me about it. The night I got trapped here, only a few park lights stayed on. It was really dark, and there were places you couldn't see anything."

"That must have been frightening!" Sue said.

"Not really."

"We should get back to it."

"You're right. Otherwise there'll be no chance of finishing."

As it was, they finished with two minutes to spare. "Look at that. We could have done at least five more," Sue said.

"Speak for yourself!" Candace rolled her eyes. "I think I need a nap. I definitely need some aspirin; my wrists are killing me."

"I hope they're not hurting tonight."

"Me too."

"I'm heading home to get some rest," Sue said.

"Sounds like a plan. I'll see you back here at seven thirty."

Candace headed home where she lay down on her bed and tried to get some rest. Unfortunately, she just couldn't fall asleep. She lay there thinking about the Scavenger Hunt and how much pizza Josh's team could possibly eat, and Kurt, and how was she going to survive the night with Lisa, Pete, and Roger. Two of them had it in for her, and the third was a danger to himself and others.

She finally got up at half past five, went downstairs, and tried to eat dinner with her parents. They were having meatloaf, which normally she really liked. It was hard to choke down the food, though. She wasn't hungry, but she forced herself, knowing she'd regret it later if she didn't.

"You excited about tonight?" her dad asked.

"Nervous more than anything," she admitted.

"Maybe it won't be as bad as you think," her mom said.

"The best thing you can do is try to have fun no matter who's on your team. Just give the best you can. No one can ask anything more," her dad encouraged.

"Thanks," she said, feeling a little bit better despite her misgivings.

After she finished eating, she decided to head to the park. At least she would be there and settled instead of home pacing the floor. When she reached the park, she found everything in a fever pitch. The normal referee entrance was closed, and the security guard standing there was directing everyone around to the main entrance.

The park had closed to players at six. Referees, mascots, and corporate types were all being corralled into the Home Stretch at the front of the park. A rope stretched across the far end of the area, cutting off access to the rest of the park. Security staff who were not participating in the Hunt guarded the rope and roved through the park making safety checks and assisting in the planting of clues.

The only other member of her team who was already there was Roger. He was sitting, pale and nervous-looking, at one of the tables in front of the ice-cream parlor. She joined him. "How you doing?" she asked.

"I'm okay," he said.

"Anything happened yet?"

He shook his head. "They rounded us all up over here. That was about half an hour ago. People keep arriving, but there haven't been any announcements yet or anything."

"You haven't seen Sue, Pete, or Lisa have you?"

"Didn't you hear about Lisa?"

"No, what?"

"She left work early, stomach flu."

"Yes!" Candace shouted.

Roger jumped but everyone else around seemed to ignore her. "What is it?" he asked.

"A miracle. We're David, and Josh's team is Goliath. And now for the first time, I actually believe we can slay that giant."

"Really? I'm not sure how, especially now that we only have four people. That's one less mind to think and remember and figure stuff out. We're almost guaranteed to lose."

Candace threw her arms around him in a spontaneous hug. "We're not going to lose, Roger. Just you wait and see. David was small but he put everything in God's hands. We may not win, but let's play like we can."

"Wow," Josh said, walking up. "You seem to have caught the spirit."

Candace hugged him next. "Lisa's sick. Isn't that the best news you've ever heard?"

"No, but I take it that's the best news you ever had," Josh said, laughing and hugging her back.

"I'm not going to die! And our team's going to win!"

"Wow, that's pretty tough talk from a team that's down one member. Care to up the wager?"

"Nope, pizza will be enough of a victory prize for me," she said.

Josh blinked in surprise. "My gosh, you're confident."

"What's going on?" Becca asked, walking over.

Becca had been avoiding Candace ever since her co-workers threatened Candace. Candace jumped to hug Becca as well. "Dear, sugar-addicted Becca. My team's going to win!"

Becca laughed. "Are you sure you're not the one who's on some sort of sugar rush?"

"No sugar, just faith. That's all David needed, and that's all we need."

"Is she making any sense to anyone?" Roger asked, bewildered-sounding.

"She is to me," Sue said quietly, having slipped up unnoticed.

Candace hugged her too. Before she could say anything, though, Sue said, "I heard. We're going to win."

"Yes, isn't that great?"

The Home Stretch was getting really packed as more and more people showed up. Everyone moved quickly, finding their teammates and huddling with them. Soon Becca moved off to find her team. Josh's team gravitated to him. They were all wearing zippered sweatshirts. Once they were all together, they unzipped them to reveal matching T-shirts underneath that said *We Want Pizza!*

"Sorry, couldn't resist," Josh said with a smirk.

Candace stuck her tongue out at him before sitting back down next to Roger and Sue. "So, how exactly is this played?" she asked.

"I'll tell you how it's played," a deep, craggy voice answered. Candace looked up and saw Pete standing there, glaring at them. "Hard and fast."

He pulled up the remaining chair at their table and sat down. "Usually the first thing they give you is a list of questions you have to find the answers to. When you do, you turn your list in to your designated Game Master and they give you a clue. That clue will take you somewhere in the park where you'll find your next clue, and that will lead to your next. Each team gets the same number of questions and the same number of clues. But not everyone gets the same ones, or if they do, in the same order. The first team to complete their challenge and make it back here to the Home Stretch wins."

He looked slowly around the table at each of them. "I've been on the winning team the last four years. I hope you've all been paying careful attention to everything you've seen in this park."

"What are the boundaries?" Sue asked.

"You can only go where players can go. No going off field."

The crowd began to quiet suddenly. Candace stood up and tried to see, but there were too many people in the way. Finally, she heard a woman's voice, which she recognized as Martha's, coming through a bullhorn.

"Okay hunters, if you haven't found your group, report to the nearest Game Master. We're the ones wearing the red sweat suits. I want you to form rows, starting here at the front. Teams 1–10 make up the first row. Teams 11–20 make up the second row, and so on. Once you're lined up, Game Masters will be by to tie you to your teammates. If, during the course of the Hunt you need to use the restroom, report to the restroom by the Painting Wall in the Kids Zone, by Kowabunga in the Splash Zone, or by The Temple of Hermes in Greece. There Game Masters will assist you in disconnecting and reconnecting from your teammates. Any other disconnecting is forbidden. Any team found without all its members connected will be instantly disqualified. Now take your places."

"What number are we?" Candace asked.

"One hundred forty-three, all the way back by the gates," Pete said. "Now would be the time to use the restroom. Go now or forever hold your—"

"Eew!" Candace and Sue burst out together. Then they both took off running to the bathroom by the front gate. A minute later they returned to stand next to Roger and Pete in the last row.

A Game Master came up to them after a couple of minutes. "Team number?"

"Team 143," Candace spoke up.

"Names?"

"Roger."

"Sue."

"Pete."

She hesitated only a moment and then said, "Candy." It was her theme-park name, and it was time to embrace it.

"I have Lisa down as home with the stomach flu. That puts you a man down."

They nodded. She handed them each a heavy nylon belt which they buckled around their waists. Each belt had a solid ring on the front of it, and through this ring on each of their belts she passed a rope, allowing for about two feet of slack between each of them. She tied the rope off on the two end rings. Pete was on one end, with Candace next to him, Roger on her other side, and Sue on the other end. How she got stuck between Pete and Roger she wasn't entirely certain, but the deed was done.

Martha hailed them all again through the bullhorn. "Your list of questions is being passed out to you now. Do not open them. On my signal, the front row will open their lists and begin their Hunt. After one minute, on my signal the second row will open their lists and begin their Hunt, and so on. Each row's starting time will be noted and taken into consideration when making the final tallies."

That meant that Candace's team would be starting fifteen minutes after the front row, where Josh and his team were. Two rows ahead of her, Candace saw Becca with her teammates. They looked like people from the bakery; Candace recognized Gib.

She didn't know which row Kurt and his team were in. She didn't even know who was on his team, but she thought it might be some of his roommates. It would make sense.

The Game Master returned to their row, and Candace was shocked to see that she carried a box with cotton candy in it. The exact same cones that she and Sue had been making up earlier. She heard Sue groan.

"No way," Candace said. "Martha had us making those up all morning. She said it was for a big game over at the stadium."

Pete laughed. "Every year it's always something clever, and every year they pick new refs to do their dirty work unknowingly." When the Game Master reached them, Candace took the cotton candy. It was only right.

Martha went at it again with the bullhorn. "Okay, first row. Go!"

Shouts filled the air, and Candace counted three balls of pink sugary fluff as they were tossed into the air. "How rude!" She had worked hard to create that; someone should at least have the decency to eat it.

"The questions are wrapped inside the cone," Pete said.

"So I figured."

"Row two. Go!"

More cotton candy went flying. The remaining rows took three quick strides forward as they moved closer to the front.

By the time they sent off row five Candace's stomach was churning with anticipation. Her hands had started to sweat, and she wiped them impatiently on her jeans.

By the time row ten was off her hands had started to shake, and her breathing was becoming ragged. She saw now why everybody signed up in March. It wasn't to get a good team, it was to get good line space. Having to wait was unbearable, and the tension mounted as each new row was sent off.

"Row twelve. Off!"

They all stepped forward, and now Candace saw that Becca's row was at the front. She also noted that unlike the others, Becca's team had no cotton candy. She stared, trying to figure out how that was going to work. Suddenly a security guard stepped forward and handed an envelope to Gib. He rushed to the side just as Martha yelled, "Row thirteen. Off!"

Poor Becca! She couldn't even dream of getting at the cotton candy. Or at least, that was what Candace thought until she saw another ball of pink fluff arcing through the air, headed straight for Becca's upraised hands. A moment before she could catch it, her team lurched forward and away from it, knocking her off balance. The man next to her physically picked her up and ran a few feet with her before dropping her. Candace's blood chilled as she heard a terrible screech fill the air. "Give me the candy!" She shivered, remembering what the security guard had told her about last year with Becca and the Jelly Bellies.

"Row fourteen. Off!"

And suddenly they were at the front. She could see teams running for different parts of the park. Others had only gone a little way and then pulled over somewhere to read over their papers. Two of the teams in row fourteen collided with the group from the bakery, and Candace saw Becca reaching for someone's cotton candy.

She forced her eyes to the cotton candy in her own shaking hands. And finally, she heard, "Row fifteen. Off!"

She tore open the bag. Her cotton candy tumbled to the ground to join so many others, and suddenly she didn't care because she had the stick, and as she unwound it, a piece of paper came loose and she could see the first question.

21

They all crowded in around her to read the paper in her hand.

Question One: How many men signed the Declaration of Independence?

"Fifty-six!" Candace shrieked. Sue handed her a pen and she wrote it down, silently thanking Kurt's history lessons.

Around them teams were running like crazy, shouting questions to each other and arguing about the answers. Candace forced herself to tune it all out and focus on the words before her.

Question Two: How many sit-down restaurants are in the History Zone?

"We need to find a map," Sue said.

"No, we just need to think," Candace said. "There's Aphrodite's."

"King Tut's," Roger said.

"No, that's a buffet, that doesn't count as sit-down," Pete pointed out.

"There's King Richard's Feast in the medieval area, that makes two," Candace said. "At Poor Richard's Pub you order at the bar, so that doesn't count."

"Smith's Tea Shoppe is table service if you're having high tea," Pete pointed out.

"Okay, we'll count that one as three," Candace said. "That leaves the Wild West area. The Chuck Wagon and the Saloon aren't table service. So, three?"

"Isn't there a restaurant on top of the fort?" Sue asked.

"Yes, Boone's. It's not open to the public, though," Pete pointed out.

"I say we count it," Sue said.

"So, four for sure," Roger said.

Candace wrote down *three open to the public plus Boone's*. Everybody nodded agreement.

Question Three: How many types of muffins are on the menu at the Muffin Mansion?

"We better get over there and count," Pete said.

"No, hang on, I know this," Candace said. What was it Becca had told her that first day they'd met?

"Seventeen! No, wait. That was before the poppy seed ones."

"Do they still carry those?" Roger asked skeptically. "After all the trouble they caused."

"I think so."

"But you're not sure?"

Candace shook her head. And then they all turned and looked at Pete.

"We have to save time on running if we possibly can. Put down eighteen including poppy seed," Pete said.

Candace wrote that down.

Question Four: Name four mascots from the History Zone.

Candace didn't even stop to talk. She just wrote: Zorro, the Lone Ranger, Robin Hood, and Ben Franklin.

Question Five: Besides sports cards and memorabilia, what personal item can you get at the Dug Out?

"Oh, that's me!" said Roger. "It's vanity cards with your picture and stats on them."

Candace wrote that down. They were halfway through, and so far they hadn't had to go looking for an answer. She hoped their luck held.

Question Six: What is the actual name of the Twirl and Hurl?

"Oh, I know, Atomic Coaster!" Sue said.

"Correction, it's *The* Atomic Coaster," Roger said.

Candace wrote it down.

Question Seven: How many women's restrooms are open to players?

"Twenty-seven and I clean every dang one of them!" Sue shouted.

Question Eight: How many train cars total are used in The Zone?

"Twenty-two," Pete said.

Candace wrote it down.

Question Nine: What is the song that plays in the Kids Zone?

"I Want Candy!" she screamed while writing it down.

Question Ten: Where can you see the Founding Fathers?

"The colonial area," Roger said.

"Too obvious," Pete said.

"Oh, I know. That's the show at the big theater in the Holiday Zone!" Candace said.

She wrote down *Holiday Zone Theater.*

There was one last line on the paper.

GO THERE!!

"What does that mean?" Candace asked.

"It means, run!" Pete yelled, already in motion.

In a moment they were all running toward the Holiday Zone as fast as they could. When they reached the theater, the main doors were open and they dashed inside. On the stage was a Game Master, sitting in a chair and calmly waiting.

"Team number?" she asked, as they thrust their sheet of paper at her.

"Team 143," Roger said. Candace glanced sideways at him, amazed that he had run all that way without incident.

The woman wrote their team number on the top of the page and then picked up an envelope from a stack. She wrote something else down on the paper before handing them the envelope.

"How many teams before us?" Pete asked.

"Only one. From now on, you'll be following Treasure Track 5B. Good luck."

They ran back outside and then stopped as Pete ripped open the envelope. They read the message in bold letters: **Humpty Dumpty sat on the wall. Humpty Dumpty had a great fall. And all the king's horses and all the king's men couldn't write Humpty Dumpty again.**

"There's nothing about Humpty Dumpty in this park," Roger said.

"Maybe it has something to do with fairy tales," Pete suggested.

"It's wrong," Sue said. "It should end with 'couldn't put Humpty Dumpty back together again.' The 'couldn't write Humpty Dumpty again' is wrong."

There was something tickling at the back of Candace's brain. She could feel it, but couldn't quite put her finger on it.

"Maybe it's in some kind of code," Roger suggested. "Or maybe only some of the words mean something."

"That's it—the word *write*—I wouldn't expect it to be spelled that way. That doesn't mean to set him right, but to write something about him."

"Humpty Dumpty sat on a wall, fell off, and they couldn't write anything more about him. What does that mean?" Pete asked.

"I think Roger is correct. There are only two words here that are really important: *write* and *wall*. It's the Painting Wall!" Candace said.

They turned and raced to the Kids Zone, dodging several other teams as they went. There on the Painting Wall was stuck an envelope marked 5B. Candace grabbed it and tore it open.

She read, "He rode fast, long, and hard, and yet he did not carry this sword."

"Oh, oh, I got it!" Sue shrieked. "The sword ... King Arthur ... the one in the stone that you have to pull out!"

There was a moment of silence before Pete grabbed her by the shoulders and shook her. "Pull yourself together, woman, that's at Disneyland!"

"He rode fast! It's got to be something to do with Paul Revere!" Roger yelled.

Before he could finish his sentence, they were all off running. There was a jerk and the rope stretched taut before Roger starting running too. They ran toward the History Zone, all four abreast. They entered the medieval area and then raced along the edge of the river until Paul Revere's Ride came into sight.

"Now what?" Sue asked as they came to a halt in front of the carousel.

"Does one of the horses have a sword carved into the saddle?" Candace asked.

Without warning, Pete plunged through the turnstile, causing the rest of them to stagger and nearly fall before passing through as well. The carousel was in motion, spinning around as it played a tinny rendition of "Yankee Doodle Dandy."

"Does anyone know how to turn it off?" she heard Roger ask.

Candace was too busy staring at Pete to answer. "What are you doing?" she asked.

Pete was standing right next to the carousel, leaning slightly forward with hands loose at his side. Then, without warning, he sprang up onto the revolving platform. The rope pulled tight through the ring on Candace's belt, and Roger staggered into her. Pete's hand snatched at something on one of the horse's flanks, and then he jumped back off. He held out his hand and in it was a carefully folded bit of paper.

"Wow! Nice going," Roger said admiringly.

Pete only shrugged as he opened the paper.

"Bask in the applause as you make it to the end zone," he read.

"The End Zone is the exit. That's not very specific," Sue noted.

"The applause must be the clue," Roger said.

Candace felt like the answer was right in front of her, but she couldn't put her finger on it.

Pete just shook his head. "I can't think of anything having to do with applause close to the exit."

"Applause, clapping, cheering. They do some of that at the games in the Game Zone," Sue said.

"Yes, but that's not close enough to the exit," Pete said.

"Can I see it?" Candace asked. Pete handed her the paper.

"Bask in the applause as you make it to the end zone," Candace re-read.

"*End zone* is a football reference. Maybe it doesn't mean the exit, but something to do with football," Roger suggested.

And suddenly she knew exactly what it meant. "It's the Spiral!" Candace shrieked, louder than she had meant to. "Come on!" She turned and everyone ran after her.

"They yell 'touchdown' and the crowd cheers at the end of the ride," she panted.

"All right, way to go, Candy!" Pete said.

When they reached the ride, Pete and Roger pulled ahead and made for the entrance. The rope tightened and Candace reached out and grabbed it, yanking to get their attention. "It happens at the end of the ride!" she shouted. "We need to go through the exit."

The guys turned, and racing slightly ahead of her and Sue, they ran up the sloping ramp. At the top they came out on the platform and stopped so abruptly that Sue and Candace ran into them.

"Where?" Roger gasped.

Candace looked around wildly. The ride was shut down for the evening, and the cars were neatly lined up in the station.

"The cars are the footballs, so let's check them," Pete suggested. They started with the rear car and worked their way forward, looking for something. Suddenly Roger gave a shout.

"What is it?" Candace asked.

"Never mind," he said after a minute, pointing to an envelope taped to the nose of one of the cars. "It says team 3E on it. We're team 5B."

"This has got to be the right place, though, let's keep going," Sue urged.

Taped to the nose of the first car they finally found an envelope with 5B emblazoned on it. Sue grabbed it and ripped it open.

"It says, 'Love is in the air and this cupid has felt it too.'"

"That's got to be at Aphrodite's," Roger said.

"You've got to be kidding me!" Sue said with a groan. "That's all the way on the other side of the park, and we were just over there."

"It's a test of endurance just as much as anything else," Pete said, already on the move and causing the rope that connected them to pull tight. Candace took a deep breath. In a moment they were all running again, this time down the exit ramp and back toward the History Zone.

It was harder getting back to the History Zone. More teams seemed to be leaving or entering it than before. Candace watched as three teams tried to thread the needle only to nearly throttle two people and land everyone in a heap on the ground that Candace and her team had to run around.

When they made it inside Aphrodite's, they discovered at least ten other teams there as well. "You've got to be kidding!" Sue gasped.

Every cherub in the room had an envelope taped to it.

"There must be one for every team," Roger said.

"Start at that end," Pete said, pointing to the one where the fewest people were clustered. It was a lucky choice; a quarter of the way down the wall they found their envelope.

"To play the impossible game and to win a dog of incredible size," Pete read. "It sounds like a parody of 'The Impossible Dream' from *Man of La Mancha*."

"But it's referencing my first Zone miracle," Candace said. "Let's go!"

They followed her, not bothering to ask where they were headed. She led them straight to the Game Zone and to the game where she had won Happy. "It's got to be somewhere around here," she said.

They searched for a full minute before Roger gave a shout. Candace saw that he was pointing at the glass bottles. Barely visible, several envelopes were peeking out of the tops of bottles. To get close enough, they all had to vault the wall. Candace cringed as Roger went over, having a vision of him crashing into the entire display of glass bottles, but he landed just fine.

"It's this one here," Sue said, yanking an envelope free. "Take your trophy and head to the finish line. You'll find it locked up in 223. Just don't forget the Swingers' leader."

"Locked up sounds like a locker to me," Roger said.

"With the number, definitely," Pete said.

"Where are the player lockers, at the front of the park?" Candace asked.

"Actually, there are several scattered all over, usually close to the restrooms," Sue said.

"So, where is Locker 223?" Candace asked.

"Problems, Cotton Candy?"

She turned around to see Josh. "Nope. We've got everything under control," she assured him. She and her team hopped back over the wall.

"Glad to hear it," he said. "See you in the Splash Zone later." He winked at her, and then his team climbed in to search for their own envelope among the bottles.

Something about that wink gave her a hunch. "I think I know where to find our locker," she said and began to run.

"Where are we going?" Pete asked.

"The Splash Zone."

It made sense. There were loads of lockers in the Splash Zone so people could lock up their cameras and other valuables before going on the water rides. She was sure Josh had been giving her a hint.

They found the lockers in the Splash Zone and, moments later, number 223.

"How do we get it open?" Roger asked.

"The guest lockers are opened using one of these central computers," Sue said, pulling them over to the one nearby. "You put in your password, and it opens your locker."

"How do we know what the password is?" Roger asked.

"It's got to be in the rest of the clue," Pete said.

"Just don't forget the Swingers' leader," Sue re-read.

"Well, the Swamp Swingers sing with Freddie McFly," Candace said.

"The codes are five letters. It's got to be McFly," Sue said. She punched it in, and there was a buzz as their locker opened.

Inside was a miniature trophy. Candace grabbed it out. "To the finish line!" she shouted.

Back outside they had to weave around several teams that were growing increasingly agitated. At last, the finish line was in sight! A large, white chalk line had been drawn at the entrance to the Home Stretch. Another team came running from the direction of the Game Zone, steps ahead of them.

Roger gave a shout and leaped ahead, yanking the rope taut and literally propelling the rest of them forward faster. The other team began to run faster, but one of their members was limping, holding them back.

Candace and the others passed them and then raced over the finish line, shouting in victory. She held their trophy aloft and ran straight to the small cluster of Game Masters with clipboards. She presented them their trophy.

"Team 143 following Treasure Track 5B. We were in the last row, so I think we just won!"

The Game Masters were all grinning broadly. They took down the time and their team information. "We won't know who won until all the teams have come in and the questionnaires have all been scored. But congratulations on being the first team back!" Martha said. "Go have some ice cream and relax."

They turned in their rope and belts, and then Candace and her team staggered over to the table they had all been sitting at earlier. Roger went inside and returned holding four large glasses with ice-cream sundaes. He set them down gracefully on the table.

Pete clapped his hand on Roger's shoulder. "Good work tonight. To all of you," he said, including Sue and Candace in his gaze. "You really pulled together, and I'm proud to be a member of this team. I just wanted you to know that."

"Does that mean you won't try and run us down?" Roger asked hopefully.

"I never said that. I'm still going to try and run you down. But with the speed and grace you showed tonight, boy, I have no doubt that you'll be able to evade me for many years to come."

Roger turned slightly red but looked pleased.

"It turned out we didn't need my flashlight," Sue said, pulling it out of her pocket with a laugh.

"But we might have. Good thought bringing it," Pete said. "You're a smart girl."

"And you," he said, turning to Candace. "I think you'll find a home here."

Candace was surprised. "But I'm not looking for a home," she said.

He winked. "I think you are, and you just don't know it yet."

"To us," he said, raising his sundae in salute.

They all clinked glasses and then began to eat. Candace turned to watch as Josh's team staggered across the finish line. They turned in their trophy, rope, and belts and then limped toward Candace and her team.

"You have got to be kidding me," Josh said, eyes wide.

Ten minutes later Becca's team crossed the finish line through what appeared to be the sheer effort of her will. It was like watching a tug of war—all of them were trying to hold her back and yet she moved forward at an alarming rate, pulling the rest of them behind her. Gib had a look of terror on his face. A closer look at Becca's face revealed the reason. There was pink sugar all over her lips and cheeks. Strands of cotton candy seemed to be stuck in her hair, and bits of wet cotton candy were crusted on her fingertips. Becca was a cotton candy monster come to life.

It took almost two hours for the rest of the teams to trickle in. Ten minutes after that Martha was back on the bullhorn. "We've tallied up your times and added five minutes to it for every wrong answer on the questionnaire. A full list of results will be posted tomorrow morning in the Locker Room. However, we are ready to announce the three winning teams now."

A loud cheer went up.

"In third place with a time of one hour ten minutes is team 7, aka We Want Pizza!"

Josh's team jumped up and down and Josh accepted a large trophy from the Game Master next to Martha.

"In second place with a time of one hour 6 minutes is team 113, or the Please Don't Feed Becca team!"

Becca's team, ragged as they looked, still gave a mighty cheer. Becca ran up to accept the award and did a little curtsey. Someone had obviously managed to get her to a bathroom and had gotten most of the cotton candy off of her.

"And in first place, with an *astounding* record time of only 52 minutes, is a team with one seasoned pro, two rookies, and the klutziest guy in the whole park—team 143, We Love Cotton Candy!"

Pete gave her a shove, and Candace ran up to receive a massive trophy. Everyone cheered and applauded and she bowed and then waved the rest of her team up. They stood together and bowed. Josh's jaw was hanging open, and all his teammates looked dismayed. Candace held the trophy high above her head, stuck her tongue out at Josh, and did a victory dance.

22

Candace woke up slowly, one thought on her mind. It was her last day of work. Somehow that thought seemed so strange. How could it be over already? In many ways it seemed like the shortest summer vacation ever. She glanced toward her dresser at the little trophy that glistened there, engraved with her name. The large one her team had won was engraved with all their names and already stood in The Hall of Fame in the Home Stretch. Next to her dresser sat Happy. The huge dog was actually taller than her dresser.

She got dressed still feeling the strangeness of it all—the last time wearing the pink and white striped blouse, the last time wearing the white skirt. And as she put her fingernails through a pair of pantyhose and had to throw them away, she hoped it was her last time having to buy them in bulk.

As she headed for the front door, her dad put down his morning paper. "Candace, come here a minute," he said.

"What is it, Dad?"

"I just wanted to say congratulations. I think you came through your first job with flying colors. It's a big step, and it's a hard one. You had a lot of stuff thrown at you, but I'm proud of how you handled it all."

He stood up and gave her a big hug.

"Thanks, Dad," she said, grinning from ear to ear.

"No problem, honey. Oh, and your mom said that tomorrow the two of you are going shopping for school clothes."

"Awesome!"

"Have fun."

She left the house, and as she got into her car she thought about what a strange day it was so far. She drove to the park and found herself humming "I Want Candy" nearly the whole way. All summer she had looked forward to this day with excitement. But as she parked in the employee parking lot and showed her identification to gain entrance to the park, she felt a little sad instead. "I've got my emotions on backward," she said. It was something her father sometimes said, and it made sense to her for the first time.

She checked in and found that her cart was over in the Splash Zone. She hoped Josh was working; she had forgot to ask him if he would be. It would be nice to say good-bye to some of her friends. Of course, it was silly to think that way. Some of them, like Becca and Martha, worked at the park year round and she could see them anytime. Josh didn't, though, and she didn't want to miss saying good-bye to him.

Walking toward the Splash Zone, she came to the railroad tracks. She looked and saw the train coming. She dashed across. It might have been her imagination, but she could have sworn that Pete slowed down slightly.

"Strange day," she said to herself.

"Cotton Candy, wait up!"

She turned and saw Roger running toward her. She cringed, waiting for him to trip over something. He didn't, though, and he came to a standstill next to her, grinning from ear to ear.

"What's up?" she asked him.

"I tried out for my school's soccer team and I made it!"

"Roger, that's wonderful!" she said, giving him a quick hug. "Congratulations! I told you you could do anything you put your mind to."

"I know, thanks. It's weird. Ever since the Scavenger Hunt, everything just seems, I don't know, different somehow."

"That's really great."

"Is today your last day?" he asked.

She nodded.

"Mine too. But I'm coming back to work at the Scare Zone. You should totally do it too. You'd have so much fun as a maze monster."

"Yeah, I could just see that," she said, pretending to bare her teeth and claws.

"Perfect! You have to do it."

"I'll think about it," she said with a laugh. "At the very least I'll come see you."

"It's a deal. Gotta run."

He hurried off, and Candace watched him go, amazed at the transformation. Maybe it was true that sometimes all people needed was a little self-confidence or a little encouragement. She just prayed he didn't get hit in the head with a ball and end up permanently damaged. "Strange day indeed."

When Candace got to her cart, Martha was there waiting for her.

"Something came for you today," Martha said.

"What is it?" Candace asked.

Martha opened her hand, and there was a brand-new name tag that said *Candace*. Candace stared at it for a second and then began to laugh. "You have got to be kidding me! On my last day? That is just so wrong!"

Martha was laughing too and wiping at her eyes. "I thought you'd appreciate that. I mean, better late than never!"

"Oh my," Candace said trying to catch her breath. "That's a good one."

"You want to wear it?" Martha suggested.

"No, I don't think so. I've been Cotton Candy all summer, and it just seems wrong somehow to try and change now. I will keep them both, though, to remind me."

"Of your time here?"

"No, that sometimes it takes time to get what you want."

"Sometimes you don't even know what you really want until you get what you thought you wanted," Martha added.

It was a solemn moment. Too solemn. They both started laughing again. Candace took the pin and slipped it into the pocket of her skirt. "Believe me, I'm going to treasure this."

"I'm going to miss you," Martha said.

"For a while there I wasn't sure I was going to make it," Candace confessed. "In fact, I'm sure I wouldn't have without all your encouragement and good advice."

"For a while *I* wasn't sure you were going to make it," Martha said with a smile. "But I knew you could, and you stuck with it and really made a great go of it here. We could use more like you."

"Who knows, maybe I'll be back next summer," Candace said. It was strange to admit that out loud, but she had been thinking about it all week.

"That would be just fine. We would certainly be glad to have you back, and I'll make sure and say so on your end-of-play evaluation."

"Thanks."

They embraced and Candace felt her throat start to constrict. It was going to be harder leaving The Zone than she had thought. "Well, I'll be back to visit," Candace said when they pulled apart.

"You better. We've got all the great events coming up, especially for Halloween and Christmas."

"I wouldn't miss it," Candace said.

Martha nodded, smiling, and then turned to go. It was just as well because Candace was afraid she might start crying otherwise.

It was a good thing it was a slow day, because she seemed to be all thumbs as she wound up a cone for a harried mother of three. The woman didn't seem to notice or care, though, and went on her way with sticky candy tendrils dangling everywhere.

Candace turned away and saw a familiar figure marching resolutely toward her. It was Becca with a bakery bag clutched in her hand.

"I'm sorry it's your last day and not just because of the cotton candy," Becca said. "I brought you this—chocolate with chocolate chips."

"No poppy seeds?" Candace joked.

Becca rolled her eyes. "We've done thorough testing and modified the recipe so you should be able to eat five a day without a problem. Still, just to be on the safe side, I thought you'd like the chocolate."

"Thanks, that was sweet."

Becca shrugged. "So, what are your big post-Zone plans?"

Candace laughed. "Sleep in for the next week before school starts and get some shopping in. I was working here to earn money for summer, and I didn't have the time to spend much of it."

"Still, you had fun, right?"

"Yeah, I did. Crazy, strange, scary fun."

"Then you're an official Zoner."

"What does that mean?" Candace asked.

Becca leaned close. "It means you'll be back," she said with a wink.

She turned to go and Candace stopped her. "Wait. Don't you want some cotton candy?"

Becca's eyes went wide and her lips began to twitch. "You don't have to," she said.

"It would be my pleasure. Besides, I won't be here tomorrow for your co-workers to yell at."

"Thanks," Becca said.

Candace wrapped as much cotton candy around the cone as she possibly could. It was the biggest, stickiest work of art she had ever created, and Becca took it from her gently, reverently, with a crazed look in her eye.

"You are my hero," Becca said before turning and running off.

Josh finally showed up, and he looked serious. "What's up?" she asked him.

"I don't want to get involved, but I think you should talk to Kurt before you go."

Her heart skipped a beat. "Why?"

"He's going nuts. He wants to talk to you pretty bad, but I think he's afraid to," Josh said.

"Why would he be afraid to?"

"I don't know, but he's been acting pretty weird lately. Just go talk to him, okay?"

She nodded. She had been trying hard to put Kurt from her mind, with little success. When her lunch break came she headed over to the History Zone, nervous, but resolute. If he had something to say to her, today was the day.

He was the Lone Ranger, just as he had been that first day they met. Her breath caught as he turned and looked at her. He rushed over and pulled her to the side where they could have a little more privacy.

"Don't say anything, just let me get this off my chest first," he said.

She nodded.

"I've been thinking a lot about what you said, and you're right. I do need to think about my future."

"Kurt, you don't need to say that just for me."

"It isn't just for you. It's for me too. What you said makes a lot of sense. I can't be a costumed character forever. I want to have a real life, and I want you to be part of it."

"What are you saying?"

"I care for you, Candace."

"You do?" she asked. It was the dumbest thing she could have said, but it was all she could get out around the lump in her throat.

"Yes, and I want to prove to you that I can be the man you need."

"I'd like that," she whispered.

He bent down and kissed her and it felt so good. She could have stayed like that forever, but he was the one who pulled away.

"I've signed up to take the high-school equivalency test, and I'm planning on starting community college next quarter. Nothing big, I'm just going to get my feet wet and see where it takes me."

"I'm proud of you," she said, not knowing what else to say.

"Will you consider giving us another chance?"

She nodded, not trusting herself to speak.

"Great. I have to get back to work now. Maybe we can discuss it more tomorrow night, over dinner?"

Again she just nodded.

He kissed her quickly. "Gotta run."

Strange day indeed!

When she went back to her cart, Josh looked relieved. "Everything cool?" he asked.

"I think we just got back together," she said by way of answer.

He grinned. "That's great! Congratulations."

"Thanks."

"Now all you have to do is come back to work Scare. You should, it would be a lot of fun."

"That's not that far away," she said.

"No. You should hurry. If you want one of the good monster jobs, then you have to sign up by—"

"Let me guess," she said sarcastically. "March."

Josh grinned at her. "No, this week."

"Oh," she said, shocked that for once she wasn't late for something at The Zone. "Are you going to be working the Scare Zone?"

"That's the sweetest part. I'm going to be a vampire in one of the mazes."

"Cool."

"You should totally sign up to be a vampire chick. They get the hottest costumes," he said with a sly wink.

She felt herself blush. "I wouldn't want to wear anything too revealing."

He shrugged. "You could always be a mummy."

"What's the down side?" she asked, suspiciously.

"Their costumes are so hot and constricting that at least one faints every weekend."

"Great. Any other options?"

He grinned. "Ask the recruiter and find out."

"I think I just might," she said, rising to the challenge. After all, it would only be about six weekends. And it would mean extra spending money. Where was the bad?

Josh smiled as though he could read her mind. "See you in three weeks, Cotton Candy."

Yeah, but then maybe you'll be calling me something else, like Candy Corn, she thought.

The afternoon flew by, and when her final shift was almost done she thought she might cry. She gave Josh a big hug and made him promise to IM a lot. "And don't forget, you're taking my team out for pizza on Saturday."

He rolled his eyes. "You know, you were so excited, I was just trying to encourage you. I had no idea your team was that close to winning or I never would have helped you."

"There's only so many lockers in the park. We would have won with or without your help."

"Oh yeah. Prove it."

"I might, but you'll just have to wait until next summer."

"You're seriously planning on doing all of this again next summer?" a familiar voice asked.

Candace spun around to see Tamara. "Hey! What are you doing here?"

"You didn't think I was going to miss your big finale, did you?"

"Thanks, Tam," Candace said hugging her.

"Next summer?"

"I might," Candace said. "We'll see."

"So, when exactly do you get off?"

Candace looked at the girl who was coming to relieve her. "In 3 ... 2 ... 1."

"I'm here to relieve you," the girl said with a smile.

"And you don't know how relieved she is," Tamara said.

Candace laughed. "Thanks."

Tamara and Candace moved off.

"So, it's your freedom day. Whatever you want to do, we'll do," Tamara said.

Candace thought for a moment. "You know, strange as it may seem, I want to go on some rides."

"You know you're crazy?"

"It's been said."

"Okay, as long as you know. Race you to the Glider!"

Tamara took off running with Candace close on her heels, trying to laugh and run at the same time. She'd spent the summer trying to leave this place—and now that she could, she wasn't. Becca was right. She was a Zoner.

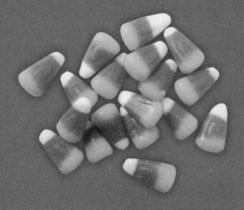

the fall of candy corn

debbie viguié

Read chapter 1 of *The Fall of Candy Corn,* Book 2 in Sweet Seasons.

1

Candace Thompson knew she was crazy. That was the only possible explanation for why, once again, she was sitting across the desk from Lloyd Peterson, hiring manager for The Zone theme park. A lot had changed since the day in June when she had been hired to operate a cotton candy machine. Still, sitting across from Lloyd, she felt self-conscious and a bit insecure.

"So," he said, staring at her intently. "You think you can be a maze monster for Scare?"

She nodded. Scare was what they called the annual Halloween event at The Zone. Aside from putting frightening elements in traditional rides, during Scare there were a dozen mazes where monsters did their best to scare park guests as they wound their way through dark and creepy corridors.

"Then show me something scary," he prompted.

It was eleven in the morning in a brightly lit office. What on earth did he expect of her? She wanted to say something smart. She wanted to say something funny. She realized with horror that she didn't have anything to say.

"Come on, come on," he said. "Be a monster; jump around, growl, or something."

She got out of her seat and did the best growl she could. Unfortunately, she sounded less like a monster and more like a frightened Chihuahua.

"Threaten me!"

She got closer to him than she would have liked, jumped up and down, swung her arms, and then pounded her fist on his desk. She could tell by the look on his face that he wasn't impressed.

She growled again and yelled, "I'm going to get you!" She felt like the world's biggest idiot. No one would be scared of a teenage girl, especially not one wearing a gray business suit and sensible shoes.

"Scream!" he ordered.

She threw back her head and screamed her loudest, shrillest scream. That, at least, was easy. It was a game her best friend, Tamara, and she had played when they were little. They had competitions to see who could scream louder or longer or higher.

She screamed for ten seconds and then sat back down in her chair. She expected Lloyd to laugh. She expected him to say something derisive. Instead he was looking at her thoughtfully.

"I have the perfect role for you to play," he said. He wrote something on an orange slip of paper. "You're going to be Candy in the Candy Craze maze."

"Candy?" she asked questioningly. "Am I going to be dressed up like a giant Twix bar or something?"

He shook his head. "Nothing like that. You should be proud; it's our latest maze. The lines for it will wrap halfway through the park."

He handed her a stack of papers. "You can go fill these out. Then, on Saturday at nine a.m., report to the costume warehouse for your fitting and orientation. At that time you'll also be able to pick up your badge, ID, and parking pass."

"Saturday at nine," she confirmed as she took the stack from him.

"There's a table — "

"Out in the courtyard," she finished for him.

Since she was a returning employee, there was slightly less paperwork this time. There was, however, an entire book of rules and policies regarding Scare. She had to sign several forms stating that she had received it, read it, understood it, and promised to abide by it. It seemed like the golden rule of Scare was thou shalt have no physical contact of any kind with players. Touching a player — a customer — was grounds for immediate firing.

Once she had finished filling out and signing all her paperwork, she returned it to Lloyd Peterson. Checking her watch, she discovered that she still had an hour before she had to meet Tamara for a late lunch. She decided to head into the theme park to see a few friends.

The first thing she noticed when she entered the park was that the Holiday Zone was closed and that temporary walls set up around the area prevented players from going inside or even getting a peak at what was going on.

The Holiday Zone was one of nine themed areas inside The Zone theme park. The theme of the Holiday Zone changed throughout the year to reflect different holidays. It was the day after Labor Day, so all the Fourth of July theming from summer was now being replaced with Halloween theming for fall. The transformation would take about ten days, and then the Holiday Zone would be open again for business.

Several key attractions throughout the rest of the park were also closed, getting their Scare overlay. The Muffin Mansion was one of them, she discovered when she went there looking for her friend Becca.

She knew that two of her other friends, Josh and Roger, had ended their summer jobs and weren't there. Fortunately, both of them were going to be working Scare. They had managed to talk her into joining them. Spending time with them was one of the best perks of working the event. One of the other perks was that it paid slightly more than her summer job had.

Martha, her former supervisor, spent a lot of time off field in the employee-only areas. Candace wasn't sure if Sue, one of her other friends, had already quit her summer job as janitor or not. That left Kurt, so Candace made her way to the History Zone.

Kurt was her boyfriend. The word boyfriend was still exciting and new to Candace. Kurt worked as a mascot, a costumed character. They had met the day she became a Zone referee and, after some rocky moments, had ended the summer as a couple.

She found him in the medieval area of the History Zone, dressed like Robin Hood.

"Hey, gorgeous!" he said when he saw her and gave her a quick kiss.

"Eeeww!" said a little boy holding an autograph book.

"She's not Maid Marion," the boy's sister protested.

"She's not?" Kurt asked, feigning surprise.

To Candace he said, "Away lady, for you are not my dearest love."

Candace pretended to be crushed and put her hand to her forehead as though she might faint. The children laughed at that. "But I am! I am wearing this disguise to hide from the evil Prince John."

"Robin will protect you!" the little girl said excitedly.

The little boy handed Candace his autograph book with great solemnity. She signed Maid Marion's name, and he seemed immensely pleased.

After the children left, Kurt smiled at her. "Nice job."

"Thank you. I'm practicing my acting skills for Scare."

"You signed up?"

"Just now."

"That's great! What did you get?"

"Apparently I'm in the new maze. I'm playing Candy."

Kurt looked startled, but before he could say anything, he was besieged by several more children wanting pictures and autographs. Soon a line formed. Candace glanced at her watch, and Kurt shrugged and gave her a smile. She waved good-bye and headed for the front of the park.

Twenty minutes later she was sitting with Tamara in their favorite ice-cream parlor.

"Want to split a turkey sandwich and a banana split?" Tamara asked.

"Split the split? You took the words right out of my mouth," Candace said.

After the waitress took their order, they began discussing the fact that they had only a few hours of freedom left before school started up in the morning.

"I can't believe we only have two classes together this year," Tamara complained.

"At least one of them is homeroom," Candace said.

"Drama should be fun, though," Tamara said.

"I can't believe I let you talk me into signing up for that."

"Come on, you're going to be a maze monster; what's a little acting to you?" Tamara teased.

Candace smiled. "I am pretty jazzed about that," she admitted. "I just hope I do a good job. I totally couldn't pull off scary in front of the recruiter today. I should thank you, though. I got a position based on my ability to scream."

"You're welcome," Tamara said. "See, all those hours in the garage paid off."

"You're going to come, though, right?"

Tamara was adventurous, but she hated anything that resembled a monster or something that went bump in the night. She couldn't stand horror films and hadn't even been able to make it through the movie Jaws the year before without freaking out and vowing never to go swimming in the ocean again.

"I guess if you're going to overcome your fear of mazes enough to work in one, the least I can do is come see you in it," Tamara said with a heavy sigh.

"You're the best."

"I know."

After lunch, they did some last-minute school shopping, and each of them ended up with pencils, paper, and three pairs of shoes.

"Seriously, I don't think I can wear these to school," Candace said, pulling a pair of three-inch black heels out of one of the bags.

"Then you can wear them after school when you go out with Kurt," Tamara said. "That officially makes them 'school adjacent' and therefore school shoes."

"You have messed-up logic, Tam, but I love it."

"Knew you would."

They headed back to Candace's house so she could change clothes before youth group. While Tamara unpacked her shoes for her, Candace threw on a pair of jeans and a Zone sweatshirt she had borrowed from Kurt.

"You're never giving him back that sweatshirt, are you?" Tamara said.

"Not if I can help it," Candace laughed. "Besides, it's the duty of a girlfriend to swipe some article of clothing from her boyfriend. It's like a sacred trust. The guy carries a picture around of the girl, and the girl snags his sweatshirt."

"You weren't even cold the other night at the theater when you got that, were you?"

"I'll never tell," Candace said with a laugh.

When they left the house and headed for church, Candace was both excited and a little nervous. Thanks to her summer job she had missed out on youth group all summer. Now she was returning, and she was officially a senior. It would be her first senior-y thing.

Once they got there and entered the familiar building, she began to relax. The youth building was large and furnished with old beat-up couches, chairs, and plenty of pillows for sprawling on the floor. Almost a hundred people were in attendance. The freshmen were easy to spot with their wide-eyed looks of excitement. They had finally entered the major leagues, and it was a big night for them too.

Candace and Tamara staked their claim to one of the smaller couches just before the youth pastor, Bobby, called everyone together. They prayed and then sang a couple of praise songs.

"Okay, welcome, everyone, to a new year. We're glad to see all you freshers out there. And, seniors, congratulations on being the top dogs."

There was a weak yell from the freshmen, which was dwarfed by the shout of the seniors. The sophomores looked relieved that they were no longer freshmen, while the juniors looked enviously at the seniors.

"Make sure you grab a fall schedule before you go home tonight. We've got a lot of great events coming up in the next couple of months. There's the girls' all-night party next Friday night. Don't forget the annual all-church marathon the following Sunday. We're going to be having a guest band at the end of the month, and I know you won't want to miss that event. We're also doing something brand-new this year. The first Friday in October we'll get on buses and head on over to Scare at The Zone!"

Cheers went up from almost everyone in the room. Candace was stunned. She knew a lot of church youth groups went to Scare, but this was the first year her youth group would go. She began to rethink her employment options. It was going to be weird enough being a monster on display in a maze without her entire youth group there to see her. Slowly, she sank down lower on the couch, willing herself to be unseen.

Tamara waved her hand in the air, and, before Candace could grab her, Bobby called, "What is it, Tamara?"

"I just thought everyone would like to know that Candace is going to be a monster in one of the mazes."

Candace could feel her cheeks burning as she glared at Tamara.

"Hear that everyone? Make sure you come with us to Scare, and you can see Candace at work!"

There were more cheers as Candace sat there in dismay.

A fresher girl raised her hand.

"Yes, what's your name?" Bobby asked.

"Jen. How much will Scare cost?" she asked, clearly concerned.

"Well, Jen, that's the best part. This is the perfect time to invite all your friends, Christians and non-Christians. The entire event, including entrance ticket, transportation, food and souvenir T-shirt, is being completely sponsored, so it's free!"

There was a standing ovation. Candace just glared up at Tamara. "This is your fault, isn't it?" she asked.

Tamara just smiled innocently. "I have to support my best friend, don't I?" she asked.

Candace thought that maybe she could use a little less support and a lot more privacy, but she didn't say so. As cool as it often was to have a friend with money, there was a downside.

"How could you do that to me?" Candace asked when she and Tamara were back in the car.

"I love you, Cand, but if you think I'm going through those mazes by myself, you're crazy. I plan on putting as many bodies between me and the guys in the scary masks as possible."

"But I'm one of the guys in the scary masks! Besides, it's perfectly safe. They're not allowed to touch players at all."

"That's what you say."

"It's true. It says so in the handbook."

Tamara rolled her eyes. "Yeah, and how many people aside from you bothered to read it?"

"That's not fair—it's in the pamphlet too," Candace protested.

"Oh, and because it says so in the pamphlet it must be true," Tamara said. "Maybe if they posted it on the web it would be doubly true."

"Knock it off," Candace said, still irritated and in no mood to play.

"Seriously, you're not worried are you?" Tamara asked, doing her best to stop smiling.

"No, I love being in the spotlight," Candace said, letting the sarcasm flow freely. "Hello! Remember me? Your best friend? I hang around with you so I can be 'spotlight adjacent,' as in, not in—but nearby."

"Well, you need the drama class worse than I thought," Tamara said.

"I don't want to be in the spotlight."

Tamara pulled her car up in front of Candace's house and parked. "You know," she said, her voice suddenly very thoughtful, "for someone who doesn't want to be in the spotlight, you seem to be spending a lot of time in it lately."

"Hello? Not my fault," Candace said.

"I'm not saying it is," Tamara answered, putting her hand on Candace's shoulder. "I just think you seem to end up there no matter what you do. I mean, you were a cotton candy operator all summer, and how many times did you name something at the park or win some competition or otherwise draw everyone's attention your way?"

"Too many," Candace muttered.

"Exactly. Stuff like that doesn't just happen. I think maybe God's trying to tell you something."

"Like what?"

"Like maybe you're not meant to live your life 'spotlight adjacent.' Maybe you're meant to be front and center."

Carter House Girls Series
from Melody Carlson

Mix six teenage girls and one '60s fashion icon (retired, of course) in an old Victorian-era boarding home. Add boys and dating, a little high school angst, and throw in a Kate Spade bag or two ... and you've got the Carter House Girls, Melody Carlson's new chick lit series for young adults!

Mixed Bags
Book One

Softcover • ISBN: 978-0-310-71488-0

The Carter House residents arrive shortly before high school starts. With a crazy mix of personalities, pocketbooks, and problems, the girls get acquainted, sharing secrets and shoes and a variety of squabbles.

Stealing Bradford
Book Two

Softcover • ISBN: 978-0-310-71489-7

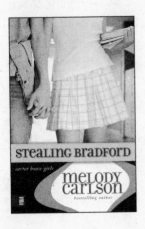

The Carter House girls are divided when two of them go after the same guy. Rhiannon and Taylor are at serious odds, and several girls get hurt before it's over.

Books 3–8 coming soon!

Pick up a copy today at your favorite bookstore!

Forbidden Doors

A Four-Volume Series from Bestselling Author Bill Myers!

Some doors are better left unopened.

Join teenager Rebecca "Becka" Williams, her brother Scott, and her friend Ryan Riordan as they head for mind-bending clashes between the forces of darkness and the kingdom of God.

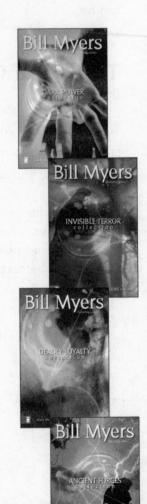

Dark Power Collection
Volume One

Softcover • ISBN: 978-0-310-71534-4

Contains books 1–3: *The Society, The Deceived,* and *The Spell*

Invisible Terror Collection
Volume Two

Softcover • ISBN: 978-0-310-71535-1

Contains books 4–6: *The Haunting, The Guardian,* and *The Encounter*

Deadly Loyalty Collection
Volume Three

Softcover • ISBN: 978-0-310-71536-8

Contains books 7–9: *The Curse, The Undead,* and *The Scream*

Ancient Forces Collection
Volume Four

Softcover • ISBN: 978-0-310-71537-5

Contains books 10–12: *The Ancients, The Wiccan,* and *The Cards*